—T┐ STARS THAT NEVER SHINE

Making of an NFL football player

Stay Blessed
Joe Harris
#51

BY JOSEPH A. HARRIS

J & J PUBLISHING

ATLANTA • NEW YORK • NORTH CAROLINA • LOS ANGELES

THE STARS THAT NEVER SHINE

Making of an NFL football player

Published in the United States of America.

ISBN: 978-1-60414-187-0

A trade paperback book.
For book orders, author appearance inquiries and interviews, contact Joseph Harris at Joeharris51@hotmail.com

Library of Congress Cataloging In Publication Data

This publication states the events that occurred from my personal point of view. The purpose of this document is not to malign or discredit any individual or organization. It has been written primarily for the purpose of an autobiographical account and "teaching commentary" with historic significance from the author's perspective.

Fifth Revised Edition

Fifth Edition literary coaching: W.C.A. Development

TABLE OF CONTENTS

Acknowledgements

Special thanks to Shawn D. Lytle, Claudia McRae and Arthur Roberson who encouraged me to write the book initially and provided invaluable advice and literary support. Special thanks to my long time friend and accountant, the late Luther Harris.

My hearty thanks to literary consultant, Aduke Aremu. Also, to Dawn Alli and Cherice Kirkland of Dove, LLC . Special thanks also to Ed Shoemaker for editorial contributions and to Carl Agard CEO of Adelphi Publishing and Media Group for publishing consultations. A very special thanks also, to the W. Calvin Anderson and www.facebook.com.

PROLOGUE — MY CAREER

I was blessed to earn the opportunity to play in, Super Bowl XIV. Playing in the Super Bowl was a very long way from where I started out. It was a great experience, even though we (the Rams) lost against the Pittsburgh Steelers (final score 31 to 19).

I had the honor of being the Special Team Captain! I have always held my championship Super Bowl ring near to my heart.

It is a source of great pride because, "I had gone all-the-way" in a game that requires a lot of discipline. Plus! I had to carefully manage my career for many years, to stay on the field and because of that I have played historically with the some of the best professional athletes in the game of football.

My career in sports got underway because I was wise enough to work towards graduating from E. E. Smith Senior High School in Fayetteville, North Carolina. From E. E. Smith Senior High School, I was fortunate to be recruited to play college football on a scholarship at the Georgia Institute of Technology in Atlanta.

I was inducted into the Georgia Institute of Technology Hall of Fame in 2000 and that was one of my most profound accomplishments. I still hold the record for making the most tackle's in one season for the school. After graduating from Georgia Institute of Technology with a degree in business, the Chicago Bears then drafted me in the seventh round in 1974. Also drafted that year was the great legendary Walter "Sweetness" Payton! He was drafted in the first round. I played for only one year with the Bears.

Following My Career and Making It Happen....

I then moved to Ontario, Canada to play for the Hamilton Tiger Cats. There I played for two years with one of the fastest players in Canada, out of Dallas, Texas. The player's name was Dave Shaw. I was honored to serve as the Captain of the Team! While playing with that team, I would go to Texas each summer to work out with Dave and Hollywood Henderson.

The coach for the Tiger Cats was an astounding man by the name Bob Shaw who was known for his toughness and intimidation of players. From there, I was recruited by the Washington Red Skins by Coach George Allen. He was the Head Coach back then in 1977.

He chose two players out of Canada to come back to the N. F. L. from the Canadian league. The other player was Joe Theisman, quarterback for the Toronto Argonauts. After playing for one year, I was headed to California to complete the promises that I had made to my mom and to myself (I will explain later).

Pete McCullough was one of the coaches with the Washington Red Skins and landed the position of Head Coach for the San Francisco 49ers. He decided that I was what they needed to complete their defensive line and took me with him. I was Captain of this Team as well.

I had the honor of playing with wonderful players such as, Willie Harper, Archie Reese, Freddie Solomon, Cedric Hardeman, Al Collins and "The Juice", 0. J. Simpson for the next year and a half.

I moved yet again, to Minnesota, to play for the Vikings under Coach Bud Grant. Bud Grant was one of the nicest men I have ever player for and it was one of best opportunities I ever had. He appreciated players very differently from all the others. I played with legends like, Chuck Muncie, Jim Marshall, Ted Brown, Mac Blair, Fred McNeil and Nat Wright!

I left Minnesota because I was placed on something called "waver wire" when the coaches brought back a veteran player by the name of, Paul Krause.

I was then, picked up by the Los Angeles Rams by Bud Carson, who had recruited me at Georgia Tech. Bud, was then the Defensive Coordinator for the Rams.

His notoriety was enormous because he developed defense called "the steel curtain" for the Pittsburg Steelers. He and Ray Malovasi, head coach for the Los Angeles Rams wanted me back in California! I stayed with the Rams from 1978 to 1983, playing with distinguishing players like Drew Hill, Kent Hill, Wendell Tyler, Billy Waddy, Cullen Bryant, Pat Hadden, and Jack Youngblood.

I also played with Fred Dryer, Pat Thomas, Rod Perry, Phil Murphy, Jackie Slater, Dennis Harrah, Lawrence McCluchen, Ron Jesse, Preston Denard, Eddie Hill, Bob Lee, Frank Carrel, Larry Brooks, George Andrews, Greg Westbrooks and Hacksaw Reynolds!

I moved on from there to Miami, Florida to play with Dan Marino, Don Bessillieu and Wally Kildenburg for the Dolphins. Don Shula was the head coach.

Next, I chose to move on to Baltimore to play for the Colts and within a year I was traded by the Colts back to Washington, D.C. to play in the league known as the U. S. F. L. (U. S. Football League) and there I played for the Washington Federals.

My last and final professional team assignment was with the Memphis Showboats in Memphis, Tennessee. During my career, I recovered fumbles and I scored throughout my career.

As you review my career you can see, that life for me was always subject to a "career move." A professional ball player must learn how to manage change. I will also explain why I was traded so many times and hopefully you will understand how profound the role of "industry and team politics" is in professional football. When you watch pro sports in the media you don't get clear perspectives of the lifestyles of many of the players. Most of the television and media coverage is just the glamorous parts of the pro sport's lifestyle.

Secrets of Success

S – start by determining your ultimate goal in life
E – establish your priorities to reflect those goals
C – create a plan that includes room for flexibility
R – research and practice to reduce risks and errors
E – efforts lead to rewards, excuses lead to failures
T – time used wisely is an investment for the future
S – strength is achieved by confronting difficulties

O – organization, focus, & persistence gain results
F – faith in Jesus frees you from fear and doubt

S – self control is the truest test of human mastery
U – use your talents and skills as natural resources
C – challenges always offer opportunities for growth
C – change is the only constant you should depend on
E – experience exceeds all other methods of learning
S – society never owes you more than you have earned
S – success is a way of life found moment by moment

Dedication

This book is dedicated to my
Beloved Mom and the rest of my family ...

IN THE BEGINNING

IN THE BEGINNING

My life's story begins with my grandparents on my mother's side of the family. I never knew much about my father's people. I grew-up in a small town where everyone knew one other. We lived in Apex, North Carolina most of the time with my grandfather.

I was named after my granddad. My grandfather was a sharecropper who later became a great businessman. His name was Joseph Alston. For my entire childhood I lived with my parents and grandparents between two cities, Apex and Fayetteville, North Carolina. Fayetteville was not very far from Apex. It is geographically is located just outside of a neighboring city called Chapel Hill, North Carolina.

Joseph Alston, my granddad, was a good-looking man. People often mistook him for a Caucasian, but he was actually half-Native American and African American. I remember he always thought that "mistaken identity" was funny.

He didn't mind people *mistaking* him for one race or the other, but he was most concerned, about people appreciating him for the fact that he was a fair and a nice person.

My grandparents had three boys and one girl. Their only daughter was my mother, Mattie Mae Alston. Like I said, I didn't really get to know many of my fathers' family. They weren't around much and I was "the quiet child of my family" and I didn't ask a lot of questions. Back then, "children were seen and not heard."

I never, "questioned why", about anything. I just figured that if I was supposed to know something, then the adults would sit me down and explain things to me. I thought I had all that I needed anyway, growing up. My grandfather, Joseph Alston owned one-hundred and twenty-six (126) acres of farmland. On his farm we grew tobacco, collard greens, corn and green beans.

There was also lots of livestock, cows, goats and beautiful horses. What I remember most, is the beauty of granddad's horses. On the farm, we had all kinds of nice people working. There were African Americans, Native Americans, as well as Caucasians. Not only did they work the land, but they lived on it too as a community.

My grandfather was very handsome and he had a head full of beautiful hair. He was very tall and slender with some of the most gorgeous eyes "you could ever see." Granddad was very religious; he would sit all day sometimes listening to the sermons of his favorite ministers, Reverend Ike and Oral Roberts.

He would also send money to support their ministries every single week. His commitment and dedication to do this taught me about the purpose of paying church tithes. I didn't fully understand what it meant back then, but as I got older I found out what he might have gotten in return.

He insisted that I be a respectful child and that I grow to be a strong and respectable man. He ordered that we all do what he considered "the right things." This included obeying our parents and following Biblical rules concerning life. I guess that is what made me the man that I am today. Grandpa was strong and he lived like a wise and strong man.

Other Family Members...

I had a lot of other colorful family members also. One cousin, who was named, Richard ran home-made liquor or "moonshine" throughout the winding roads of our home county. I remember that he could drive his, excuse the expression, "tail off." Why, Richard could drive faster backwards, than most people could drive forward. He had friends like the Petty's, the family of the great race car driver, Richard Petty.

They too, cousin Richard, led me to believe "drove very well also for all kinds of reasons" all through the winding roads of North Carolina and raced with my cousin Richard. My cousin (to let him tell it) won the backwoods racing between the families most of the time and sometimes had to do some stunt-driving backing the car up in reverse. He would tell me stories about how even the law would "hem him up in a corner" and he would back the car up so fast, he'd get away.

Even to this day, I think of cousin Richard, when I see Burt Reynolds on television with his *Bandit* stunt-driving sequels. Our Richard was definitely a bragging kind of man. The stories he told would captivate me as young boy and I would admire his wit and his apparent physical strength.

I would just stare, marvel at his confidence, muscles and stories. All of my cousins and uncles had great physiques and I know that they got their muscles from working on the farm.

Farm work was very hard work. It built mind, body, plenty of discipline and patience. Down the street from my house lived a couple of my cousins named Willie and Obe Ford who were very slim guys. Willie was one of the best masonry men ever to go through the course at our school. He was a *jack of all trades* and *I was jack of all sports*. My cousins would always come to my house and eat up all of our food. They would walk in the door with a smile on their face but we all knew they came to eat. We were one big happy family.

MY BIRTH

MY BIRTH

At the time of my birth, my mother was on her way to visit some family members in a little town called Pittsboro, North Carolina, located between the cities of Fayetteville, and Apex. While on her way to her cousin's house she went into "child-labor" very early in the morning on December 6th, 1952 in the middle of the Pittsboro Town-Square. Fortunately, for both of us there was a doctor's office just on the left side of Town-Square.

I was born in the center of town. I must have always been destined to make some news! During slavery, it was right there in that square and center building that slaves were bought and sold. The square is considered an historic site. I hoped that my birth would one day represent positive memories for the town. Today I am a proud member of the Fayetteville Sports Hall of Fame (inducted in 2009).

As I stated earlier, I spent a lot of my formative years on the farm that my grandfather owned.

The house that we lived in would be considered small today. But back then, it was a pretty good-sized house.

My mother was a very strong willed woman. She was a beautiful black woman with long, straight black hair.

She was a loving and caring person with the most pleasant smile I have ever seen in my life. Not just because she was my mom. She made everyone that she ever spoke with feel good. Mom really was gorgeous with Native American features that were bold and expressive. My mother married my father, James Harris at a very young age. He was an Army man and, "one of the best Chefs to ever enlist into the U.S. Army." Dad stood about five feet ten inches tall and was a stern built man with somewhat of a violent temper. He often drank alcohol heavy — and that's when his temper would flair. Between the two of them, they had three boys and one girl, Claretta.

One of the boys was John. John lived with my granddad and died at a very young age in a motorcycle accident. He was extremely energetic and loved to play baseball.

Then there was James, Claretta (my sister), Raymond, and me. We were all very close as siblings to say the least. Although we had our arguments, like all siblings do, we loved one another very, very much. Our house had a total of only five rooms and we had five people living in it. We were somewhat crunched.

My brother and I slept in the same bed, in the same room, with our sister she on a roll out bed. Our parents had the other bedroom.

There was the kitchen, living room and bathroom. That pretty much, sums up what it was like growing up in a rural city with parents that were kind of young. Not a whole lot of money, raising three children.

I remember my granddad would have the farm hands paint the little house every summer and we had to help keep the grounds nice and neat. My grandmother's name was, Savannah Alston and she had a beautiful garden just outside the front door that extended down the walkway to the road. I can still remember her Azaleas and Lilies.

Working on the farm, we would earn $6 between my cousin Ed and me. We were *best buddies*. We would take that money and buy lots and lots of things from my granddad's store, which was located in the very house where I grew up. Granddad had candy, sodas and beers for the workers. It was very convenient and good business because it was about five miles to town where the nearest public store was located.

Everyone back then, had special talents, and all of my uncle's would say, I would someday grow up to be someone special and successful because I was very athletic and I loved to run. I would run through the woods, five miles to the store and pass by the Old Men out in front who played checkers all day long. They would also comment, "look at that Boy run, he's going to be something someday with that talent." That was great motivation!

GROWING UP

GROWING UP

As a child *growing up* in a small town, there wasn't a lot to do to *occupy one's self.* So, we relied on one another to *pass the time* each day. Six of us were good friends and we actually called ourselves a *Little Gang* because we were younger than the *Big Boys.* We figured that we had to stick together. There was, Arnell McSwain, William Henry Dobbins, Terrance Murchison, Ronnie McDonald, and the Virgil boys. All six of us were the best of friends, and yet there is something to this very day that I cannot figure out. If anyone of us was caught walking alone, late at night, *in the path* the same five friends would rob one another.

I lived in such a small town that by the time I or any of my siblings got home my father knew about what happened around town anytime we left the house. If he heard that we were robbed, he would make us go back and take back whatever was stolen from us.

He would tell us, "take a stick or a brick or something!" And then he always demanded that, we were not to return home until we retrieved whatever was taken from us. It was hard living in the country on a farm in the summer, but it made us tough and strong. This prepared us for the tough world that we live in now as adults.

A turning point for the little guys...

My big brother, James would not let us play with B*ig Boys* during the week in the field. The L*ittle Boys* could only play on the weekends. I vividly remember my big brother running me home, and, of course, not being fast enough to catch me. He ran me home because I gave him a tough time and fought him because we wanted to play on the field. I ran as fast as I could and he didn't even "come close" to catching me. One day in particular, I was determined to stand-my-ground and play on that field no matter what he said.

The gentlemen sitting in front of the local store laughed at my brother and told him that he was fighting a losing battle if he thought that he could catch me. This made my brother even madder. It wasn't too long after my stance against my big brother, that the Big *Boys* let the *Little Guys* play on days other than jut the weekends. We were allowed to play whenever we wanted to after that day. They soon found out that sometimes, *Little Boys* could take-a-stand for something we really wanted too. I say that because, it's not the age or size of a person that determines his or her skills. It's sometimes the individual's determination.

If you want something bad enough, you will work extra hard, and harder, in fact, than the next guy. This victory was a "win-win" for little guys in territory and attention. We gained an opportunity to play around and near the big boys and that by itself helped us (the little guys) out a lot. It enabled us, to learn up close — from watching the big boys play.

The little guys were then allowed to play around just to the side of them. And when the big boys were done, we were like an instant replay of their actions trying to carry-on and play our game on the field amongst ourselves.

My best memories growing up are mixed with memories of my beloved brother, John. He was my oldest brother and very outgoing. He was always *the life of the party,* so to speak. He had something to say to everyone. Everybody loved to talk to him. He was very energetic. He always had words of encouragement and really tried to treat everyone the same, no matter who or what their status was in our small community. The adults in the neighborhood recognized and admired him for this and said that it was an indication of his wisdom.

Neighborhood Kids...

There was another kid in our neighborhood named John, his last name was Mc Dean and he had a basketball hoop set-up in front of his house. I probably owe him for developing my basketball career in Junior High School.

John Mc Dean had a sort of a park like environment at his house. Many times, we would go out late at night and shoot the basketball into the hoop in *pitch-darkness*. We felt proud to be able to do that without missing. I actually thought that playing basketball would be my profession back then.

I had skills early on, in both basketball and football. One day I had the football in a game and I was running down the field and decided that I would try to just run right through the other guy who was coming at me. What fun! The other guy's name was, Walter Boone. I felt like Jim Brown and it was that experience engaging Walter that first helped me to realize how much I enjoyed the game of football.

I was twelve years old then and I wanted to become a professional football player. From then on, I strategically put activities together that were *the building blocks* to my professional dreams. I ran track, because I felt it would increase my overall physical endurance.

The regular participation and practice in all three sports gave me great running, maneuverability, breathing and stretching techniques and other conditioning. All of this was valuable to me in the game of football.

After actually playing the game of football myself, I would then go home to watch any game that was available for me to see on television. I enjoyed watching televised games and I would beg my Mom to take me to see any live games that I had even heard about. My favorite N. F. L. Football team was The Chicago Bears. Dick Butkus, to me, was *the most astounding player* on anybody's team. Jim Brown was certainly breath-taking to watch too, with his *quick feet* and *cool moves.*

He had his own way of playing the game and was *one of the most physical athletes* that I had ever known to *hit the field.* One man could never take Jim Brown down by himself! Jim was a Running Back for the Cleveland Browns. I also remember watching Willie Wood with total amazement. He played strong safety for The Green Bay Packers. Then there was Sam Huff, a Linebacker who played for the New York Giants. Of course, I also admired John Mackey with his fantastic Tight End skills. He was in the starting line-up for the Baltimore Colts. There were many, many more football heroes that *stood-out* in my mind when I was just a little boy!

Although, I was very young, I really understood the game and I was *totally into* the *playing-techniques* of each player. Every player had a way of carrying out his duties as a teammate. Each player provided, in my mind, a piece the puzzle for his professional team.

There were several actual, "plays" that seemed to be special to me. Don't ask why, but some of the plays had a magical effect on my abilities to grasp the *Wonders of Football.* I began to study the entire *Concept of Football* and what it would take to win at the game. Even though I was a young boy, the game of football consumed my every thought.

My father and older brothers found it fascinating that I was so young and so filled with excitement about football. And I was! I was content with learning more and more about it each and every play. Every step that they made on the field, I knew had a purpose.

REFLECTIONS OF
PRE-TEENAGE
DAYS

REFLECTIONS OF PRE-TEENAGE DAYS

I was very quiet as a child and did not like to *cause a stir*. But I had one incident where we were in line at school and this guy pushed me and I hit him really hard in the stomach. It scared me a little bit to learn that the young man couldn't breathe for a few seconds and that was when I learned that I could really hit someone hard enough to hurt them.

I should not have been fighting in school. The teacher made me sit-to-the-side for the rest of the "recess period." I'll never forget it.

The *trouble-maker* was not with me and I felt bad because in reality he started the whole thing and we were both wrong. I felt really confused because I was just protecting myself. Maybe I should have just told on him and it would have worked out better? Well, at least I know that he never pushed me again.

My father, my brothers and I, were all considered by others to be pretty quiet people but we all held firm beliefs about protecting ourselves. This was instilled in all of us from my granddad. My grandfather was a stern believer in *doing the right thing*, but at the same time, he taught us to defend ourselves, even if it might be wrong.

My father said (about fighting) that, "it don't take a knockdown; drag-out fight to earn respect from your opponent." He always said that, "all it took was, just one good solid lick, to do the trick!" He was right that time and I was wrong for fighting in school.

We went to an elementary school called, Newbold Training School. The school was about ten stories tall and looked just like a large square box with lots and lots of windows. It had a small cafeteria aside of the "humongous" square building.

We had to walk to the school each day and we would walk along the railroad tracks and through the woods to get to it. I used to fall off of the rail tracks and hurt my ankles. I had fallen so much that I still have scars from those tracks today.

My mother worked at the school. She was a Cook there. She made certain that my friends and I would all have plenty of food. It was there that I met my best friend, Charlie Baggett. Charlie Baggett, now is the former Offensive Wide Receiver Coach for the University of Washington. At recess, Charlie and I would hold foot races amongst ourselves. Charlie and I would always tie. He helped me to find out how fast I could run.

I met Dr. Martin Luther King Jr.!

One of the most memorable occasions of my life was when I heard and met the late and great Dr. Martin Luther King, Jr. I was actually at a rally listening to him. This is how that happened.

Some very kind college students from North Carolina State University were working for the local, *Head Start Program* and invited a few of us to go on a ride to a rally in Raleigh, North Carolina. I was supposed to be on my way to church at the time, but I *snuck and rode* with them anyway.

Hearing the voice of Dr. Martin Luther King, Jr., gave me a sense of pride. The way his voice rang out above all and the words that were spoken made me feel good about being a Black American. During that time in history blacks were just starting to be recognized as citizens. I will never forget Dr. King.

At the rally, I also had the distinct chance to see the Ku Klux Klan. They had on bright colors and B*oy' oh Boy, it was a sight to see!* Then all of a sudden, the Klansmen, literally started chasing the black members of our group from Fayetteville. I ran through the park and they just kept on coming.

I was so scared that I ran as fast as my legs would carry me and tried to hide behind a Bank. Luckily the local police were staked out across the park behind the Bank.

When they heard the commotion the Police asked me why I was running and I pointed back and said, "Do you see all those hooded people?"

I got a whole lot of attention that day. I became famous in Raleigh, North Carolina. I even got television coverage. That was the first time I was on national television. Sounds great huh? Well it was also the day that I got my "butt torn up" by my mother for skipping church to go to the rally. That was the one, Sunday that my momma had decided, not to attend church, for some reason and was watching television and the news.

And there I was, just as bold as daylight, being interviewed by the television News Reporter because I was singled out by the Klansmen to scare and to chase.

Playing, fighting, competing for attention and describing my neighborhood...

One day, while playing football, a guy named, Dent Reader gets the ball and runs. When he ran, I caught him and hit him so hard that I *knocked the wind out of the two of us.* I even knocked "myself" incoherent! It wasn't until we were all riding back home (which was about thirty miles away) that I realized *who I was* and *where I was.*

It was *the neighborhood store* that I used to love to run five miles to that jarred my memory.

There were actually two stores in the City of Fayetteville. One was the candy store and the other was called the *Juke Joint*. The *Juke Joint,* as we got older, had more than just candy. It had beer and corn liquor for those who preferred the hard stuff.

The other store was almost like a super market for your mom's, regular shopping items. It had things for dinner like bread, can goods, milk etc.

There was a lady named Mrs. Levy who lived a couple of houses up from us and she was head of the Church Prayer Club. She was also the Church Bandleader. I was a part of the church band also, that is until Mrs. Levy tried to teach me to play the Clarinet.

She tried and tried until we both finally discovered that I had *no musical abilities*. Walter Boone on the other hand, was one of the guys in our *little gang*. He lived across the street from us and he loved to play the drum. He would keep the whole neighborhood awake at night by playing those drums. He was a part of the Band at the Church too.

Kids and Customs...

Everybody in our gang wanted to be the leader, as is probably the case in any other "group situation."

Someone always wants to be the head, the *Honcho*, the *only one in charge*. That was a role that, *my Boy*, Arnell McSwain, wanted, and sometimes claimed! Growing young men in particular, in my little gang and in my city had a strange system for getting to do things first. For instance I remember our sort of, "welcome wagon policy" for meeting new girls.

Now every guy wanted to get the first chance to talk to any new and pretty girl in the neighborhood. New girls were like prizes and to have *a new person* and a 'fresh new face' seen with you, man 'oh man. You could claim the new person as your "new" girl and that was *real status* and local news for weeks.

So, the young guys would compete to see who would get the honor of calling such a girl his own and we fought one another for that right.

The guys would meet in the back yard at a certain time and then — the fight would be on. The winner would win the privilege of being *the first official caller in the neighborhood*. What a Welcome Wagon!

We used to roller skate down the steep roads to see who could reach the bottom first. I remember falling down the hill while skating and I slid about fifty yards! My skin was completely raw. This didn't stop me. I got right back up and tried it again. This taught me *never to be a quitter* and to this day, I still live by that and almost all those ideas were instilled in me, as a kid.

One Christmas I got a B-B- Gun and my father told me not to aim it at *anything living*, but being *the Boy that I was*, I would go out and shoot birds in the back yard when my father wasn't at home. We called this "skeet shooting." But I never let my father know what I was doing or he would have beaten my behind.

Growing up in a religious family, we were taught that A*ll of Life is Sacred.* But little boys will be little boys, and I did grow up to understand how wrong my actions were.

Another Christmas, I woke up and Santa had brought me a brand new set of weights. I was the only kid on the block who had a real set. We were very blessed to have loving parents who took the time out *to make a fuss* over us and to *discipline us* without "sparing the rod," so to speak.

Neighborhood Fun...

Our gang would build homemade go-carts from wooden boxes and old tricycle tires. We would try to see who could build the fanciest and the fastest vehicle. We used a piece of wood for the brake mechanism and sometimes they worked and sometimes they didn't.

We would also just fall down the hill on the roller skates jamming underneath and had many embarrassing collisions and wrecks on those go-carts.

I must add that I wanted also to become *a positive role-model* someday and I started early in my life trying to be positive. People would say that I was crazy and obsessed with body building and conditioning my body at a tender age. I was very determined to be strong and conditioned. I would challenge the boys in the gang to see who could lift *the most weights*. The competition would always come down to Charlie and me in the end. And though we were always competing with one another, we never let it stand in the way of our friendship. Each morning before school, I would lift those weights and try to concentrate on all of my muscles. I would repeat this in the afternoon when I would come home from school and then again before I went to bed at night.

My nickname was "Mr. Muscles", because I looked like Tarzan! You can only imagine what I looked like with all of those muscles and I was really considered short back then before I finally grew to be more than six feet tall. I never paid much attention to that nickname but as I look back, I can truly say that I was in great shape.

I succeeded in reaching one of the goals that I had set. I wanted to develop an almost perfect body and I had it.

JUNIOR HIGH SCHOOL DAYS

Junior High School Days

I attended and graduated from Washington Drive Junior High School. I had to walk around a major highway, a paved road, and then, cross a busy street (at the light) and get through a whole neighborhood to get to the school. As I would come around a curve in the street, there on the hill was, Washington Drive. The school was a flat-roofed two-story building. It had five sections to it and in the back was a big, open, red clay field. We practiced football in the back field. The gymnasium was located in the front of the school.

My closest friends in Junior High were Charlie and Henry Dobbins. Henry was a very close and dear friend to me, just as Charlie was, only in a somewhat different way. We were so close that our families treated us the same. I would go to his house and his Mom would care for me and feed me just like I was one of her own children.

I was considered a gentleman and a student. I was very popular with my teachers. I was appreciated by all of the girls.

I was despised by all of the boys — especially my teammates at the school. What more could a guy ever want? I had a great and balanced life.

By seventh grade, I was trying out for the first organized basketball team. During my junior high school years I played both basketball and football. I remember practicing all day — the day before try-outs, and most of the night. That is *until my mother made me get my "butt" in the house.* I shot at the *hoops* hundreds of times, hardly missing a shot.

See, growing up, we played in the dark because the older boys had first dibs on the court, as well as the field. You can imagine the skills that came out of our neighborhood. I had an outstanding shot for a man of my stature! They would often say, "look at this thick strong man with a soft touch." My whole objective as a big basketball player was to be able to move with the style and grace of a smaller man with a gentle touch.

I took my conditioning very seriously even at such a young age. I took pride in the fact that I had always wanted to be the best athlete that I could possibly be. I found great comfort and joy while competing in all sports. At the try-outs, the coach, Jake Willard, made us shoot the ball 50- times. Charlie and I didn't miss one shot! The Coach would eliminate you if you missed, or if you *looked like* you 'didn't have what it took' to be on his team. He was a tough coach! The coach had cut most of the boys on the team. It got down to two of us and he decided that I shouldn't be on the team.

I remember I begun to cry and complained that I hadn't missed a shot and Charlie backed me up on that , so the Coach had me and the other boy, the one who was also to be cut, *go to the free throw line* and make 25- shots. The other guy had missed several of his shots during the course of the day as well as the shot at the free-throw line.

The coach still felt that I was the one to be cut, mainly because the other guy came from a richer neighborhood. I was from the Evans Hills. We were the outcasts, even though we all attended the same school, it came down to *neighborhood politics.*

That's when I first experienced that politics can easily come along with a sport and as a young person, I couldn't fully understand why.

I did eventually *make the team.* I ended up even being the captain and the highest scoring player in the whole division. I scored so many points that the score keeper would pass off my points to the other players. My best friend, Charlie Baggett was also one of my teammates. He was quite a player himself and one of his good friends was the statistician, the person who noted which player scored each point. His name was Julian Brown.

It was said that for every 6-points that I made, the next 6 were given to Charlie or James Lee. I guess that's part of the politics that is endured with sports! I didn't find this out until I had entered college. Some of the guys told me that they did this because they were jealous of me.

I was a good team player even though I endured a lot of ridicule.

I was labeled an outsider. I was still a very humble guy. Never bragged, I kept my confidence intact and I *stayed to myself* and I had one heck of a seventh grade year!

This was except for the time, I recall bringing home my report card and I made a "D" on it. My father really put his foot down and said that I couldn't play basketball. I was so hurt, especially after all that I had gone through just to make the team. I cried and begged and pleaded. I promised my folks that if I could get a second chance, I would change that "D" into a "B."

I wouldn't stop crying and pleading until finally my Mom said that, "I had to live up to that promise or else, I would get my butt beat and I would go on punishment for *an undetermined amount of time.*" You can believe that I "buckled-down" and made my promises good. I wasn't the smartest kid, but I did the very best that I could. There would always be someone that was willing to help me with my homework, but I never let anyone completely do it for me.

We all sometimes "try to take a few shortcuts" but I knew that if I got caught, then my father would *handle my bottom* with regard to this type of matter as if "I had stolen something." I was the kind of guy that was never negative towards anyone. I wanted to show that I could be as good with the books as I was on the field. I had to work a little harder than most, but I ended up just fine.

My father from that period on began to realize that "I was a man of my word." This made him very proud.

The same fellows that played basketball also played football at Washington Drive where, I then played, tackle and 'linebacker. There were also times when I was allowed to play in the Tight End position. Our football Coach's name was Mr. Avant. He taught and drilled *the basics and the fundamentals of the game* into me. He made me a successful professional ballplayer. I didn't realize this at the time. But as I became a professional, I often thought of him and how hard he was on us, and how angry I was then.

If you made a mistake on the field, Coaches would give you a paddle on the butt.

I can remember once, when I first started playing in the Junior High School League. I didn't get to play in the first few games. I would roll around in the dirt to get my uniform dirty so it looked like I had contributed. In my earlier years it hurt a lot that I wasn't given the chance to prove myself, but things worked out for the best.

Many people in the community were impressed by my basketball skills, but were ten times more impressed once they got the opportunity to see me in action on the football field. I was nick-named, the *brick wall* at times by some of the players who would come into contact with me on the field. This is how politics are, in the sports.

Say for instance William Henry Dobbins' was just as good as me to go Pro but because a coach liked me and not William, then William couldn't possibly have the opportunity to prove that he was good, if not better than me in the Pros!

This was a special time in my life. I guess you could say that these were *my growing-years*. It's funny how the things that we learn as children can have such a profound affect on us as adults. The most important things that my parents instilled in me as a young child made me "the Man" that I am today.

MIDDLE SCHOOL

Running:	Laps — 5-10, an eqiuvalant of 2 miles
Diet:	Ate "everything at that time!" Steaks, Fruit, Bananas, Milk, Orange Juice, Apple Juice, Beans, Hot Dogs, etc.
Drills:	Back-ups, Redirects, Back peddling, Side-to-Side, the Flats
Weight Training:	3 sets of 15 reps, Curls, Bench Presses, Various Chest and "Lat" Exercises

JOE'S TIPS ON TRAINING & DIET

LOOKING BACK

Looking Back

As a young man, the heroes of R&B music were singers like: *Joe Tex, James Brown and The Mighty Delfonics*! You were *a lucky kid,* if you got tickets to these shows. The kids would envy you and try to start some kind of trouble because of jealousy.

Fighting for the right to love...
And early heart throbs...

There was this girl that I really liked and Ronald McDonald liked her also. He was supposed to be one of the toughest guys in our gang. That was *until he decided that he wanted this same girl* and *challenged me* to a fight in his back yard. I wasn't going to "punk-out' or not show-up, so I went and *took care of business* and *took home the glory*! All of the spectators cheered me on in disbelief that I had, "kicked Ronald's butt."

He not only was the toughest, but one of the oldest members of the group. That day, I not only won the girl, but I also won a lot of respect from the neighborhood kids. My very first girlfriend's name was, Joyce Getty. This was during my junior high school days. I really liked her a lot. She was sexy to me, if sexy is a part of a Junior High School student's vocabulary. I recall kissing her on the front steps at her house almost everyday of our romances. We would sit sometimes "necking" and sometimes "kissing" until it was *almost-time* for one of her parents to come home from work. She is now a principal at one of Atlanta, Georgia's more prominent schools.

Another girlfriend, Stephanie McKinney had a younger brother named Quentin. I shared with him many of my ideas about "body building" and "weight training." This information was influential enough to make him successful in football at Appalachian State University located in the mountains of Boone, North Carolina. He was an honor student and an outstanding football player.

I received a lot satisfaction, encouraging younger players, in my neighborhood to become "better athletes and people." It made me proud that they would listen and mimic my style of play or my ways of conditioning my body.

Stephanie McKinney's parents had a great deal of respect for me. One summer, her parents gave me the responsibility of taking care of their home while they were going on a trip. They were very pleased with my level of responsibility. I carried out the responsibility of watering the plants, taking in the newspapers each morning, as well as the mail each day. I checked and made sure that the doors were locked and saw to it that no one entered the premises.

Popularity was one of the prizes for being a good athlete. You could have two or three girlfriends and even a few special privileges at school. I say that because "good football players" aren't treated like the average person.

The bad side of that coin is that football players sometimes "go off the deep end into troubled waters!" Football players back then "acted-out" a little also. When going out with the guys some would lean towards doing things that were not legal, drinking and smoking for example.

Fortunately for me if my behavior ever started changing, my family provided some *reality checks. I remember for example that* my sister told my father that I had taken a pack of Lucky Strikes cigarettes of his. My father *tore my tail up* something awful. I wanted to kick my sisters' butt for lying on me, but I didn't. I took *my whipping like a champ.*

I started picking up some other habits that dad didn't mind. As a young kid, I loved reading books also. I read books about "successful athletes" to learn more about sports. I read books to understand how successful athletes thought. I read books about, Sam Huff, (former player of the New York Giants football team), Chris Hamburger and Dick Butkus, a former player the Chicago Bears. I always wanted to be called "The Little Dick Butkus." He was a lean, mean, "tackling machine." Watching him, made you feel like you never wanted him angry at you, especially on the field. Boy, "he was a sight to see!" I admired his strength and ability to trample anything that got in his path.

Soon after that I got a chance to see right in my own neighborhood a true Champion, the World Champion Boxer, Floyd Patterson drove down our street to see one of his family members. All of the kids ran down the street following the car. This was an exciting time for us and he told us that "if we worked hard enough we could do anything." On a few occasions we got the thrill of seeing people *that really made it* and it seemed to reduce our appetites for doing silly things after seeing *people of real stature.*

There were only a good handful of us who did extraordinary things with our lives after growing-up in "Evans Hills."

The Gang that spent most of its time doing "open-field" gymnastics...

Our little gang would occupy our time by running through the fields and turning flips. We were like gymnasts. We would turn flip after flip, some with no hands others with one hand. Oftentimes, we would compete to see who could turn the most flips. Yes, I grew up with some very physically challenging young boys who loved sports of all kinds.

Often we would blame one another for misdeeds just to get each other in trouble or to cover our own behinds from *getting a licking*. My father *didn't take to people who would snitch* on someone else. I often got blamed for many things that I had nothing to do with. But, I guess this is what most of the youngest siblings endured. I was still always "the nice guy" and no *hard feelings* to my sister for telling my father that I was smoking and I hadn't.

She perhaps in the long run may have done me a favor because I really thought twice about smoking and to this day, I never touched a cigarette. Maybe, just maybe, that butt whipping was a good thing after all.

Melvin Henderson....

I remember a young man by the name of Melvin Henderson who connected with me when I was around 9 or 10 years old. He and I attended the same church and we spent a lot of time there together. It was in church that we bonded quite differently from all of the other guys that were in our "little gang." He wasn't part of all of our little *devious and mysterious shenanigans*. He was different in a good way!

Later Melvin went on to go to Brown University and on to Duke Medical School. He in fact today is a successful entrepreneur and retired Obstetrician in Fayetteville, North Carolina.

Melvin was a scholastic genius! He was *skipped through* many different grades, I guess, maybe, that's why he seemed so different from football, jocks. He is the kind of person that you never want to lose contact with. To this day, we call each other regularly and keep up with what is going on in one another's lives. He turned out to be a real close friend! I figured out that our "connection" was due to the fact that we both had a church commitment and major dreams and aspirations of becoming successful.

A WORKING BOY

A Working Boy

Everyone in our household had a job as soon as they were old enough to work. My brothers were much older and began sooner than I. When they went to work in my younger days I also tried to find odds job and I worked diligently on improving myself through "weight training." I stayed busy like they did. I also actually worked wherever I could. I would get odd jobs like cutting grass or raking leaves. My very first serious job was at Esquire Barber Shop located on Murchison Road. I was a shoe shine boy.

I remember one week, I was having a hard time making any money and one of the barbers said, "Hey Joe! Why don't you tell them that you'll give them a free shine! This should give you the chance to prove that you can put a shine on a pair of shoes that spit would reflect from!" I tried his tactic and sure enough, *it worked like a charm*. I would shine shoes for nonpaying people, just as though they were paying customers. Some of them "tipped me" and then there were others that paid-me in full! I was so proud and amazed that it really worked!

Of course there were those who did take that "free shine", but even they became regular customers that returned each week and paid me what the shine was worth. I made more money that week than I had ever made before in my life. I learned a lot from that and it proved to be a *tremendous lesson* to me, even to this day about *just getting started.* It is the little things in life that you might not realize at the time, but these are the things that eventually *really matter* in your life.

Next door to the barbershop was a restaurant and occasionally, I would go over there to help out in the kitchen. I would wash dishes. I really didn't mind working as long as it didn't interfere with my *staying focused on my training* for my ultimate dream.

My second real job as a young adult was one that my brother helped me to get. It was at a grocery store where he was the Butcher and I started out as the store's bag boy. My brother and I made sure that our family had food on the table. We bought some of the *best choices* of meat, because we cut it ourselves. Soon after that, I advanced in the store to the Produce Section and then to the Stock/Shelf Boy. Eventually, my brother taught me how to cut meat in the back.

Later in my work experience, I finally got a job at Kelly Springfield tire factory which was considered for many in my town a career job. Both my brother and my sister worked and eventually, retired from the tire factory. It was considered a good job to work at the local factory. The pay was pretty good and it made for a sound foundation for those who decided to live locally. But me, I had aspirations of becoming famous and successful in sports!

In my teenage days, I did many things to earn money. I also tried construction at one point. Construction is an art within itself. You never think about things such as manholes, do you? Well, did you know that a manhole is sometimes in excess of fifty feet below the ground surface? This may not seem deep but if you ever had to climb down inside of one then you would know that it takes a heck of a person to do a job everyday inside of one. I tried it and found that the *darkness in the deepest* part of a manhole is more frightening than the toughest of mighty linemen coming at you "full force!" After my supervisor and I realized that climbing down *wasn't my cup of tea*, they allowed me to be "shaken up" by being an "air-jack hammer man."

If you aren't familiar, then it is a machine that breaks up concrete. It was enough to shake and wake up even the dead! The power and force that is within a jackhammer is amazing!

Using that equipment helped me to get stronger and to build muscles differently than I did lifting weights. It gave an account of just why 'Mr. Muscles' was the perfect name.

I thought that if you handled tough things, then "those things" would make you tough. I was correct. This made me tough and helped me to be able to take a good solid punch.

HIGH SCHOOL YEARS

High School Years

I attended a high school that was almost an *hour walk* to and from my house. Imagine having to "walk home" after being in school all day and after a hard practice in the game of football?

There were several ways to get to the school, we could walk through the woods, go along the tracks or we could go the long way, around to the highway. It really depended on how we felt that day which would determine which route we would take. If we thought that we might get a ride, we would often take the route that would lead us to the road.

No matter how tired we were or what the weather might have been, *we did what we had to do*, and we enjoyed the trek, to and from! Seldom did we ever get a ride home, but when we did, Coach Ike Walker would allow us to ride with him in his car.

There were many different friends that would walk home with us, in those days, like, Roderick Hodges and I would walk home together. We would stop by our old favorite candy store and get candy and then from there, we would go home to eat dinner with our families and later I would lift my weights. Then it was off to bed in preparation for the next day.

Many people then treated kids like they were their own...

Like I said, "everyone in my hometown was *close to one another."* I once met an older man, my dad's age, who had graduated from the same junior high school and high school that I eventually graduated from. He would come over during afterschool practices on the field and would motivate the *better athletes* with his advice.

He had a story about *not letting one's dreams get deferred.* You see he "would-have" become one of the best baseball catchers in professional baseball, had he not chosen to stay in Fayetteville to be with a girl who he loved deeply. He would say, "Joe, I hope that you don't do what I did and stay back for the wrong reasons."

Listening to older people has a value. This advice weighed kind of heavy on my mind for a long time because, *I had fallen in love* with a young lady. Her name was, Stephanie McKinney and she was beautiful and very tall and played basketball and was a wonderful cheerleader at our school.

Stephanie was very bright and later went on to attend Spellman College in Atlanta, Georgia.

Stephanie also went on after that to serve in the military and I hear that she now resides somewhere in the Hawaiian Islands.

The *thought of not following my dreams* of playing football never entered my mind. *I really had to pursue my dreams*, but I did have hopes that, Stephanie would wait for me *to make a name for myself.* When I left for college a few years later, she promised to wait on me to come back but when I came home again after that, I found out that she was into another relationship and this *hurt me to my heart.*

Star treatment begins....

Little things... are the real "big things" in life. It wasn't until I got to my senior year that I began to get rides to and from E. E. Smith Senior High School. I guess this was partly because I was one of the "Star Players on the football team." Anyway, one day it was raining like cats and dogs, so Coach Ike Walker said that he would give me a ride home. I took the ride and he took me all the way up to my road and because of the hard rain, the road was closed off due to the flooding.

He tried to insist on trying to get me there, but I insisted on walking the rest of the way. His kindness has remained in my mind and heart the persistency that he had, just "to try to get me home and to keep me from getting wet or sick" in that awful rain storm will remain in my thoughts as long as I live. He never knew how much I truly appreciated that ride on that rainy day.

Mr. Miller was our principal and football was his favorite sport! I guess this was why we had so many big Pep Rallies that we were allowed to miss our classes to participate in. My brothers were into basketball and they were 6"4" or better and I stood only 6'2" and I was considered short. I was stocky built with skinny legs and they teased me about this. It sometimes bothered me. That is until I started playing football and my size made a statement for itself.

I was very good at basketball, but E. E. Smith, was recognized as a "Football School." So, I thought that I should go that route and put playing basketball on hold to try to prove myself on the football field. I not only proved my skills were up to par, but I wanted to show the whole "town" that I was versatile. That's exactly what I did too!

My second year in high school, I played starting linebacker and offensive tackle. I watched men on the football field like Jimmy Harvey at Winston Salem State University and got encouragement from him.

Thank God I was finally able to exhibit some of what I'd learned and was able to try to prove myself. Our coaches' names were Mr. D.T. Carter – Head Coach, Mr. William Carver, and Mr. Ike Walker, my mentor. We had one of the best teams around the state.

My sophomore years, I decided to challenge one of our toughest players on the team for his position. It was really a mission. The young man's name was John Heard. He was the toughest player I had ever seen. Nothing got in his way. He played lineman and was known as 'The King of All Linemen!' One day at practice, Coach asked, "Who wanted to go up against John?" There was something in me that made me speak up and say, "I'll do it!" I said it very strongly.

We were then *put in the pit.* The pit is the front line and you face your opponent face to face, head on. The coach then says, "hit" and you charge and hit one another!" We would clash like two bulls ramming heads. We had great players around like Eugene Carmichael and Curtis McNeal.

We hit one another as hard as we could, yeah we really went at it trying to move the other person. I had a good technique at snapping into the charge position. I would gain my leverage to the point that I would get underneath my opponent so that he had no chance at getting me to hit the ground. That is what I did to get the name of "The King"! Everybody looked up in awe as they saw me hold my ground and, not being budged!

I turned my legs in a way to cause John Heard to topple to the ground! It was so exciting! It was at that moment that the Coach and everyone else knew that "there was another King" and that I had a future in football. You could see in the Coach's eyes, the amazement and admiration. I'll never forget the gleam in his eyes. I then earned respect from the team and the community as word got out.

That, to me, was "the greatest and most exciting challenge" in my early career. This information was placed in the newspapers and from that moment on, many colleges showed big respect and interest in me. "Joe Harris" *became a real somebody* and I got a lot of recognition for being the "hard hitter" that I was. I remember playing against one of our "cross-town rival teams" and my coaches told me to *put the wood on* anyone that got the football! And boy oh boy, I did just that!

Putting the wood on someone means to place a great, heart-wrenching, solid hit to your opponent. I had a special way of putting the tremendous fear into an opposing quarterback and in the linemen that I was up against. Terry Sanford High School had a running back in this particular game that day and following the advice from my coaches, I put the wood on him.

With the terror I tried to place into my eyes and the force of my punch to the running back, when he landed on the ground, it all made him get up from the field and rush to his Coach to say, "tell that quarterback don't make me run the ball anymore. That boy is crazy! I'm not 'going let him hit me again!"

I knew then that I was doing quite well as a linebacker! That running back wasn't the first nor was he the last to proclaim my insanity on that football field! Shortly after that game, Charlie and I began to prepare ourselves to take the SAT Exam. We studied very hard and were ready when the time came to take it.

Always after each practice, we would have to do sprints, especially after a tough and growling a practice. This was thought to push you to the edge of total exhaustion, which made you stronger the next go around.

Many other times, I recall making interceptions and running them back to score a touchdown. Dick Walker, Coach Ike's other nephew (Charlie was his nephew as well) would always complain that I would steal his passes. Dick played defensive back. I would tell him, "Don't just stand there and look at the ball, go out there and get it! Don't let me go all the way!"

One day, my sister asked, "Joe, do you really know just how good you really are?" "You have all the people in the neighborhood talking about you like you are a king and how great you are on the football field," she added. I didn't know what it meant for you to be considered *the best line backer in the state* of North Carolina."

We once played against Carlester Crumpler, the father of a couple of pro football players today, and the best running back in the state back then. We played against his school in a championship game and I hit him so hard in a game, that I knocked him on his back. He was 6'4" and had legs like a gazelle. I, well — I'm 6' 2" and 210 lbs, soaking wet!

He later admitted that, that was the hardest he had ever been hit. I replied, *"It's all about the fight in the dog. If you got a lot of fight in you, you can go along way in football."* That was one of the old sayings that my older brothers and his friends would often say to one another. I then felt like one of the "Big Dogs!" I have run into him many years later and not so long ago and he quoted that same quote to me as we spoke of the good old times.

During that same conversation, I talked about an old saying that I had heard when listening to the older guys in my neighborhood, they said, it's easy to quit and harder to keep going when things get tough on the field."

To gain respect from one of the states' fastest and best running backs was a high honor to hold. Soon after that game, there were several other players on our opposing teams that also admitted being hit the hardest ever by me. Many of these war stories hit the local newspapers and I soon became "the talk of the town!"

I used to sit and meditate on "how-to and how not-to hit" a person on the field and my father would ask what was I thinking. He would *say* not to be scared, just go out there and "knock the heck out of them." That will slow anybody down! My Dad was a tough man and I always tried to do as he said. So, every time I got a chance, I would knock the heck out of someone. After I was given this advice, many players would say, "Don't give me the ball, that boy is crazy!"

That is the kind of fear that any good line backer wants to hear from opponents! And I had the talent to place fear in many of my opponents. My career was filled with intimidation, picking up fumbles and then scoring.

When I made it to the NFL, I reflected on how I played during high school and college and it affected the way I played in the professional league. I studied my techniques and the form that I used in high school and don't tell anyone — but I went back to my fundamentals. I was still able to recover fumbles and intercept passes. Exactly how many touchdowns I made during my entire career is unknown.

I dreamed of scoring and hearing the fans cheer me on to victory. These things were part of the goals that I had set long ago. *Success doesn't just happen. You have to set goals, visualize the completed actions and push to accomplish them.* I am very proud that *I've stuck to my goals. I kept my focus, maintained a positive attitude and a sense of self -control* to ultimately become successful.

Our school had a bus that we called the "Blue Goose." We traveled everywhere in that bus. It was used by all of our school's teams; track and all other sports. Mr. Newkirk was the bus driver and he was proud of the bus. It was quite nice as I think about it. It was blue and gold. Mr. Newkirk made certain that it was clean and always shiny. The bus was "tight" as they say and motivated us. The bus helped me to stand out that year, I can reflect on being the player that stood out the most. I attributed my success to the books that I had read on Sam Huff, Dick Butkus and Chris Hamburger. Those books taught me what a true linebacker was and *what the expectations were* for being *a good linebacker*. This motivated me to *strive to be the best.*

Each coach had his own way of motivating his players. My high school coach would shout out, "Who wants to be in the Mighty Five?" The Mighty Five was the front line and this is where every player really wanted to be. Up front is where everyone, always strove to be. After that practice and my desire increased to become the new king, I was on the front line for the rest of my high school years.

All during my high school days, I concentrated both on being a good student and a good athlete. I was *Vice President* of the Student Body and focused. In the end, I was chosen to be one of a few, *High School All American*, *All East Player*, *All State* and several other honors. That's when all of the hard work paid off.

Unlike most of the other football stars, I was humble and stayed by myself.

I felt that by doing these things, they would help me to achieve the goals that I had set for myself. I loved going to school. Surprisingly enough, I never missed one day of attendance through all of my twelve years going to school. Amazing Huh? I still recommend that to all of the serious minded young people that I meet.

I enjoyed getting up in the morning early and starting my day. I really looked forward to walking to school. I enjoyed it tremendously and can recall each day, no matter how cold or hot it might have been!

The pain that I experienced during football practice made me feel stronger and I really looked forward to that. This made it easy for me to get up and start each day in a positive manner. I was always one of the first students to arrive in the morning and was definitely among the last to leave the school campus after practice.

I was a hard worker in everything that I did. My father taught this to me. He taught me to believe in God and place Him first and my father taught me to give every ounce of myself to whatever I do. Thanks Dad! A lot of other players had bad habits that followed them into adulthood. If you are a serious athlete and student be very careful of alcohol, marijuana and mistreating fans of the opposite sex.

I remember Charlie and the guys would say that it wasn't good not to drink and not to have a girlfriend. I wondered why! But I'm glad that I didn't indulge. I'm thankful that I had a lot of personal discipline. I *went all the way,* my senior year of high school, before ever taking my first drink of beer and or alcohol.

After that I will even admit that I even indulged in smoking a little marijuana. I did this just so that I could fit in with the "in-crowd", but that was a bad mistake!

HIGH SCHOOL

Running: Laps — 10, an eqiuvalant of

2.5 miles

Diet: Ate "everything at that time!"

Milk, Orange Juice, Apple Juice,

Beans, Hot Dogs, Potatoes,

Tangerines, Chicken, Biscuits

Cole Slaw

Drills: Back-ups, Redirects, Back

peddling, Side-to-Side,

20-sixty yard sprints,

Buzz to the Flats

Weight   3 sets of 15 reps, Curls, Bench

Training: Overhead Presses, Various Chest

and "Lat" Exercises

additional workout pre-school & just before bedtime

JOE'S TIPS ON TRAINING & DIET

EVANS HILLS

Evans Hills

I came from an area called Evans Hills. Evans Hills was an older neighborhood with muddy, winding roads and I must say filled with very loving people. People who taught children living there certain values like honesty, respect and discipline. Evans Hills to outsiders however, was considered a place where *poor and under-privileged families* resided. *All and all,* we might have been poor, but we had food.

Most importantly, we had great parents. I would sometimes wonder why there were some students at our school who would spend most of their time in the cafeteria. They would bully others and take their food. I found out later that they didn't get enough food at home, so they had to steal food in order to make it through each day.

A lot of the athletes were from "broken homes" and from the drug-infested section of town and they were hungry most of the time. So how do you think this affected the boys once they got to the football field? The coaches were extremely hard on these boys because they lacked stamina and energy.

You never know *how well off you are*, even though you may think *things are bad* — until you see and hear the problems of others.

There were a lot of talented people who came from Fayetteville, North Carolina. There are several things that stand out in my memories of Fayetteville like the tree that I used to climb as a child; and the 'now famous' path that we traveled on from place to place and house to house.

Everyone knew and looked out for each other. This was kind of like one great big family. If you did something wrong at a friend's house then that friend's mom or dad could and would discipline you, and then go and tell your parents *what they did*. The persons' parents would say, "good, you should have whipped his butt."

I can recall going swimming naked in a creek filled with water moccasins and a snake-infested creek called Snakey Beach.

It was there that I first learned to swim. I loved swimming and it is still a favorite pass time of mine. To this day, I swim an estimated 40 laps per day!

When I go to visit Fayetteville, I still drive by that same tree that I used to climb as a kid and remember all of the good times. A place that was safe, secure and inviting. The place I still call home.

There was a guy named Daniel Virgil and he had gone swimming with us one day. He jumped off the ledge into the muddy creek and cut himself. When I say "himself'", I really do mean "himself ". Unfortunately, this cut ended up causing him to loose one of his testicles. This made all of us think twice about running and jumping off of that ledge!

I guess because of the size of the town there was not a whole lot for us to do. So when we found a thing that that we really like doing — that thing became like a specialty. It was practiced and practiced to a point of mastery and sometimes even to a point of galvanizing a professional skill.

A lot of history making talent started in the small town of Fayetteville, North Carolina. Just to name a few, Doug Wilkerson. He played offensive guard for the San Diego Chargers. Dee Hardison was a spectacular defensive tackle for the New York Giants. There was Charles Waddell who left Southern Pines, NC to play with the San Diego Chargers. And a wonderful sportsman by the name of Bob Macadoo who went on to play professional basketball. Reggie Pinkney played defensive back for East Carolina and later was drafted by the Detroit Lions

I'm certain that there were many others who also made their livings in professional sports. Even though they are not mentioned here by name, they still have my respect. During my school days, there were a lot of success stories in academics as well.

It was rough in the little town that we called home. Just down the street from our house, there was a shotgun house where at least once a year, someone was stabbed to death.

Everyday our mothers and fathers worked hard and tried to do all of the right things, living as though we were in another place and time. Next to Evans Hills, was a section of town called "Cape Fear Courts." It was one of the roughest areas known throughout North Carolina. This area was made up of people that weren't doing so well and were having a hard time. "Plain and simply, just down on their luck." I guess their anger made them hostile and mad at the world. Therefore violence played a major role in their daily lives.

But then there was an area called "Broadell Drive." This was the area in where the high school was located. It was considered the area where the people who were "well- off" lived. It has always been my opinion that wherever a person is from, will determine what different opportunities might be available to him or her. That's how politics fall into play as far as geography and zip codes are concerned.

MY PARENTS

My Parents

My mother was the primary source of my encouragement and strength. She believed in me and my dreams of becoming a professional football player. She kept up my courage. She gave me magazines, took trips to games and provided warm hugs that helped me through many "ups and downs." She was the one who stood by me when my father would try to take me away from what I enjoyed the most, football.

My father was somewhat of a violent person, especially when he was drinking. He was an extremely strict father who demanded that, "you do, as you were told!" He was mean and stern in his own beliefs. It was my mom who was there for me when I would cry if my dad would punish me by not letting me go out to play. She was the one who told me to not let go of what I believed in. "The most important thing," she would whisper many nights is, "that your father is *recognized by you to be* only 'one' of the small obstacles that you will face in your long journey to stardom."

Mom was so…right! I don't think that it was not apparent to my father early on, just how *good I truly was* as an athlete or *how devoted I was* to the game until some of the gentlemen in the neighborhood — consistently brought it to his attention. It wasn't until then that he even came to one of my games. When he finally did see me play, he then tried, in his own way, to show some form of encouragement and support.

I remember, I had an injury one day. I hurt my ankle pretty bad and my father watched me put ice on it all day and night. He knew then, exactly how dedicated I was at striving to be the best that I could be. He came to my game that afternoon and he watched how good I was even though I was hurt. I was in a lot of pain, but that still couldn't stop me from playing in the game. I think that that was when it started to "sink in his head" that I would never give up playing football.

Eventually he got the message and gave in to the fact that nothing, not even him, could stand in the way of what I believed in. I earned his respect and finally, I got the respect that I had wanted from him.

My mother died at the "early age" of forty-six years old. It was a *tough pill to swallow* for me for a very long time. Over the years, I have found peace, within myself, once I could come to realize that *she was taken to a much better place*. The kind and educating words that she offered me will be with me always. The special moments that we shared as a family will *reign in glory*. I love you Mom. You'll forever be in my heart and memory. Before she passed away, she told me "to go forth with my dreams and aspirations," and that she,"had faith that I would be blessed with whatever I set my mind to do." It was these words that made me more determined to be as successful as I could.

Unfortunately, she died before being able to see me play in the N.F.L., but did get the pleasure of knowing that I had made it to the professional league. She told me to, "go and play the game like I had never played before." It's because of the love that my mother so desperately bestowed upon me that this book is even possible. I dedicate my book to my mom with many, many thanks!

As far as I was concerned all of my life, I feared my father because of his violent temper. He was a good man, but mean! I would watch him hit my mom and, it made a sore spot deep inside of my heart. I still loved him but it was a kind of love that is hard to describe. Watching him hit and slap my mom hurt a lot. It hurt in ways that are indescribable. And for the life of me, I don't know why she put up with it for all of those years.

I had nothing but respect for him; after all, he was our dad, the breadwinner of our household and the man that my mother loved dearly. But she put up with him for reasons unknown to my siblings and me. Today, I have no respect for men, who hit women. It shows a weakness in a man's character.

My father and my family had some good times too, but I always knew to stay out of his way and everything was going to be alright. He gave me a lot of things to think about I guess. He saved me from getting into a lot of trouble out of fear of what he might think or do to me if I acted out. This is why I am the man that I am today because I had some respect for authority. For that, thanks Dad. My mother and father reared us in a way to do all of the right things.

When he died, he was about the age of sixty- eight and died in a very strange manner. He was driving down the road one day with a very young lady, a lady almost my age, when his misfortune came about. You can *let your imagination take you where it may* lead, and I don't mind if you smile. I loved my father then and I will love him when we meet again in Heaven.

BEING RECRUITED

Being Recruited

During my senior year in high school, there were several different well-known colleges that attempted to recruit me. There was Wake Forest, Duke, North Carolina, North Carolina State, Georgia Tech, Michigan State, Vanderbilt, Tennessee, East Carolina, Utah, Wyoming, Kansas, and Élon College in North Carolina, A&T in Greensboro, Shaw, North Carolina Central, and Tulane University in New Orleans, Winston Salem State and Fayetteville State were also attempting to recruit me.

I guess you say that is a mouthful, huh? And quite impressive if I might add! Although impressive in numbers, I already had a dream to become a leader at a major university, to gain the recognition that I had planned for myself based on the magazines and the books that I read about football required that I attend a white college.

Naturally, taking and passing the SAT was going to be the key to entering a white school. I was blessed to have scored high on the SAT. This gave me a lot of freedom and the opportunity to go to any school in the country. This score came from a lot of hard work and long hours of studying. I suggest that each and every person that has set high standards for themselves realize that a high SAT score is the tool that is needed to open the doors to the college campus of your dreams.

During this recruiting stage of my career, each college wanted to give me a 'big party.' They fed me all of the big steaks at some of the *name brand restaurants* and allowed the *key athletes* to take me *out on the town* in each of their cities. Of course, it was exciting to get such recognition from all of the top schools but I ended up choosing the Georgia Institute of Technology in Atlanta, Ga. Once, I was down at University of Wake Forest being recruited and Kenny Garrett, also from Fayetteville, North Carolina, was taking us around the City of Winston Salem, North Carolina. Some of the boys and I had some type of alcohol and we got drunk that night!

Dexter Pride and I were wild at the party that night. We were acting up and wrestling as though we were already past college and on to being pro-football players. We were actually tackling one another right there in the middle of the party and having a good time. Dexter was a running back and I was a linebacker and we would ram each other and say, "Here we go, here I go" to the top of our lungs. That saying was the highlight of our storytelling the next day.

Everyone was trying to get us to stop horsing around, but we were totally out of control, and that's when we both began to throw-up those wonderful steaks that felt so well going down. Only they didn't feel so good coming back up. I was so drunk that they had to place me in the back of the car because I couldn't get any fresh air. I tried to breathe, so they let the windows down and went back inside the club. They left me 'breathless' and continued on their mission to party and catch girls!

I was *sick as a dog* the next morning. One of the worst hangovers that I ever experienced! Also that hangover was the first of many during my lifetime, but it stands-out vividly in my mind today! If I knew then what affect alcohol would play on my life in later, I never, in a million years would have touched that stuff.

Anyway, back to sports…while I was being recruited at University of North Carolina, I overheard the coach and some of their players talking about Charlie Baggett and me. I recall hearing him say, "if we can get Charlie, then we will get Joe!" They knew that we were best friends, but what they didn't know was that we were smart and to put us to the challenge turned us both off.

It placed a void in our minds that they were toying with us and took us for granted. I was no sucker! I was going to prove to them that it wasn't wise for me to overhear them say that! This made me determined not to choose that school, but Charlie ended up going to University of North Carolina for the first two years of his career, but transferred to Michigan State where he graduated. I felt that it just wasn't the college for me.

Anyway, during our stay there, we had Ike Oglesby, running back, showing us around and we, of course went out to eat. I don't remember the name of the place that we ate at, but I remember having the biggest steak that I had ever seen!

It completely covered a serving platter! And to this day, I have seen some big ones, but never one that big! At this college, Ike tried to *hook us up* with some girls so that we could get the real taste of what being in college was like. From what I understood the girls on campus at the University of North Carolina *were amazing and generous*, if you know what I mean!

Georgia Institute of Technology was only given a quota of recruiting one black football player per year so, Charlie and I went there to be recruited. And, Eddie McShan, first Black quarterback in the south and Greg Horn, the first Black running back at Tech, were taking us around and showing us a good time.

I must say, we really had a great time while we were there! Eddie and Greg had put together a little party for us at the Royal Coach Hotel. Back then, it was a "big time place" especially being in Atlanta.

They rented several rooms there, and set up the party and I called up my old girlfriend Stephanie who was one year older than me. Stephanie and a few of her girlfriends came over and we had one great big party that night. It is one that I'll never forget! We partied so long that some of the girls got in trouble because they missed their curfews. I think that the girls only ended up forgiving Charlie and me because we were only in town for that weekend and flying back to Fayetteville on Sunday.

It was a long time before seeing us again, so I guess you could say that they took their punishment and we kept a good relationship.

Everybody used to say that because of Stephanie, that's why I chose Georgia Institute of Technology. But that wasn't true; I had made it up in my mind during my junior year at high school that I would go to the Georgia Institute of Technology, solely because of Bud Carson. He was a very close friend of my high school coach and when he spoke at our Senior Banquet, I was completely sold on attending the Georgia Institute of Technology.

While at the Georgia Institute of Technology it rained and I remember watching the game on television and I kept close watch on how the players were able to play on that muddy grass field! The football field was subsequently changed over to astro-turf.

The first piece of astro-turf that I had ever seen was a sample sent to me by Vanderbilt University. They were trying to recruit me and thought that the opportunity to get to play on such material might just win me over, wrong!

What amazed me was *all of that Georgia red clay*! I recall them announcing on the loud speaker that some of us had come all the way to see 'a rainy night in Georgia!' We found this to be amusing because of the old Ray Charles song, "Rainy Night in Georgia." I was allowed the privilege of meeting a lot of top athletes around the country; athletes such as, Marcus Mooney, a running back for West Virginia. He was from Shelby, North Carolina.

There was Robert Pullium who played defensive tackle for Tennessee. Charles Waddell was a tight end for Carolina. Dexter Pride from Southern Pines went to play for Minnesota.

Roderick Hodges went to North Carolina Central. He lived right down the street from me when I was growing up. There were a lot of parties, lots of good food, many girls and lot of fast times. The traveling and getting the chance to meet a lot of the top college athletes in the United States was grand, but I am proud to have chosen the Georgia Institute of Technology.

How-To Be A Prime Candidate
For Your College of Choice!

There are various qualifications that a player must have if he or she wants to be recruited to a top school. Having good grades is one of the most important qualifications. One must maintain good grades throughout junior high and high school. This is critical for your admissions recruiter and your own selection process.

You also need to be a good role model and level headed, and not too selfish or "me" oriented about everything. Be a good person and good "citizen" on the team and in your school and community. There is no college in the world that wants to recruit a player that has a bad reputation. It's a waste of money and their time because the bad reputation, can end up representing the team itself. One must learn "valuable skills on the field and off" in their sport of choice.

For me as a linebacker in football I had to master the strong stance of a linebacker or having perfect technique just as a good tennis player or golfer had to master a good swing.

I had to stay in good health and great physical condition. Not only is this a plus while being recruited, but this plays a major role in the coming years. Good health and great physical condition can and will protect you from injuries.

You also need to really love what you are doing. If you love and even adore a sport, it shows 'on the field' when you are playing it. This will aid you when it comes down to respecting the game that you seek to master.

I feel that if you have all of these qualities. I am certain that you are ready for college life and more advanced levels of practice. I would also say that Keep all of these things in mind and you will be a prime candidate for being recruited to any college that you want to go to.

OFF TO THE UNIVERSITY

Off to the University

The very first time I experienced an airplane ride was when the Georgia Institute of Technology flew me to Atlanta. I was kind of afraid but I knew that it would be one of many plane rides that would be a big part of my future, especially with the dreams that had I for myself.

Charlie Baggett, Marcus Mooney, Charlie Waddell and I were the four recruits that were allowed the opportunity to visit. We were all extremely excited to fly! Once we got to Atlanta we were escorted by Eddie McShan and Greg Horn. They were the top players of the Georgia Institute of Technology Yellow Jackets at the time. They took us around the town and showed us the campus. They introduced us to a lot of people *and boy oh boy, were we ever excited*!

As I mentioned earlier in the book, Eddie McShan was the first black quarterback in the south. He was very neatly dressed and an outstanding individual, to say the least. I had admired him from afar even before I had the chance to be chaperoned by him.

Greg Horn was the first black running back at the Georgia Institute of Technology and they called him "Touché Away!" I would always ask him for food and he would always make sure that I had enough; boy did I love to eat! I did then and I still do now! Greg was another outstanding young man whom I will never forget.

I guess you could say that we were proud to be the guests of such an outstanding university. We received a lot of attention from the coaches and professors. My girlfriend who was one year older than me, from E. E. Smith High School, Stephanie McKinney was already in Atlanta attending Spellman College. This ultimately made my trip more than worth the wait! It gave us the opportunity to see one another and we certainly "made up for some lost time", we were great friends. Once we got to the university we had time for business and time to socialize. All of us who took the trip were destined to be a part of the Georgia Institute of Technology family?

Georgia Institute of Technology was a University with only a couple of black athletes and I felt that it would be a great place to *put down some roots*. There were only a total of twenty-five African Americans that attended the school at the time that I was there! If I recall correctly, there were only a total of five black females. Were you to go to campus today, it would look to you like one of the top Black College campuses. I guess you can say that the first blacks at the Georgia Institute of Technology opened up the doors for African Americans!

I really liked the campus itself. I adored the place where we dined and ate our meals! For the Football Team our meals were free and I especially liked that part. The campus was lovely! It was well landscaped and the dorm rooms were clean and spacious.

In addition to being a great admirer of Bud Carson, the Head Coach and my high school Coach, D. T. Carter's were best friends. That helped me to succeed in becoming a part of the prestigious institution! Bud Carson graduated from the University of North Carolina .He then moved on to become the head coach at the Georgia Institute of Technology. I used to watch the Georgia Institute of Technology on television like it was a special research project. I thought that they were a good team with *lots of small players* who were very agile and fast *on their feet.*

This is what drew my attention. I thought strategically that they could use a big and tall guy like me. My size and the size of their players gave me hope that I could make the overall picture complete for the team. I knew that I had a lot to offer their organization! I would study their plays and watch their formation in awe, just imagining myself there! I wanted to be the first black defensive linebacker to play on the team! Later I would become not only the first linebacker, but, the very first black defensive player. My dreams early on really came true for me.

It was 1971 and I was one of the first blacks on the team, so the experience was new for all of us. The team members *expected a lot from me* because *I guess, they took a chance* also. I can say that I had a lot to prove to them. But because I was determined, I wasn't 'going to let them think that I wasn't *up for the challenge*! In the beginning, it was kept sort of hush, hush that I was black. People didn't know that that Georgia Institute of Technology had their first black defensive linebacker, me. Under the helmets, it was hard to tell if a player was black or white.

I guess in 1971, it was not too acceptable by the community. But it was *the day and age* when blacks were being introduced to the white colleges all around the country. Needless to say, they gradually introduced me as yet another black affiliate of the Georgia Institute of Technology Football Team.

I was truly accepted and admired by the fans once I showed that I was more than up to par to play for the team. I proved that I was an outstanding football player as well as an upstanding pillar of the community.

My only reservation ever about that Georgia Institute of Technology was and is that no black person works in the high ticket earning sports management offices at the school. I'm not just speaking of the athletic department; I'm talking about in administration for the school either. This bothers me even today! We need to have some Blacks and people of color in administrative positions. So that diverse people can have a say and make some of the concrete decisions for the futures of all of the people at the university.

There is a *75% ratio of* black players suited up for the Yellow Jackets and I feel that a change in that situation is long overdue! Once a few of my Caucasian teammates who had gotten to know me as a person asked me why I played along with the system when there was so much prejudice. I told them that, "it was my time to make a place on a team and that I would eventually advance myself because of the training into the National Football League Association!" I told them that "I was destined to be a professional football player and that if it took being belittled then that was what I would endure!"

I would then ask my teammates why they choose the Georgia Institute of Technology? They would say that their daddies made them come. They said that their fathers had graduated from the Georgia Institute of Technology and that they wanted to keep the tradition! I hope what I said was a positive influence to them. I believe this to be true because shortly after that conversation, and after our four years at college, there were several players who became professional athletes. To name a few: **Billy Shields** went off to play for the San Diego Chargers. **Randy Rhino** went to play for the Montreal Alouttes, and **Steve Raybell** started playing for Seattle Seahawks. I'm certain that there were others too.

The white boys on the team were given the opportunity to play for the distinctive Georgia Institute of Technology team because their fathers and fore fathers prepared a path for them to follow. The black players, however had no past heritage at the Georgia Institute of Technology, therefore they had to make a name for themselves, and to prove that they were worthy of being a part of such a prestigious institution! The classes were not the norm. They were extremely hard for a person like me who had a problem with retaining all of the information.

There were many different considerations that arouse for a white institution to pick up a black football player during that period of time. There are the income standards of the player, as well as the requirements to maintain a certain grade point average academically. There are the community values that a player or person must have in order to possess the standards that a significant and outstanding player must maintain.

Imagine coming from an environment where a student has nothing but his family and barely the necessities that life requires. As compared to the white guys who had everything at their "beck and call": all the way down to a path or pattern that their fathers and therefore fathers laid for them! Again, politics! Politics not involving gender, but race! I endured all of the challenges that the 1970's had to throw at me! I fulfilled all of my dreams and aspirations! Thank you Jesus!

I remember this one game, I took a cut because my knees were hurt and the coach knew it. I should have been off somewhere soaking my knees or putting ice on them but the coach had other things in mind for me. He made me play in the game and I ended up tearing the cartilage in my knee from the wear and tear of the game. I was pissed and in a lot of unnecessary pain, which could have been avoided had my coach put the color of my skin aside and done the right thing by letting me sit out that game.

Remember earlier in this book, I discussed politics? Well this is a fine example of the kind of politics that accompanies athletics. The day that I hurt my knee at practice, my new girlfriend, the late Mary Beard was at that practice. I had often told her not to ever come to watch my practices because if I became cut or something, it would be troublesome to me, not to mention, embarrassing! I knew that my knees were getting weak and I just felt that it would not be a good day for me on the field and sure enough, my knees gave out on me. But the coach still insisted that I play in the next game! I was so upset!

This was something that was going to happen anyway because I had signs that my knees were weakening, but I was still upset! Even though I was hurt and injured, I still had one hell of a game that day. I made a couple of outstanding plays that is sure to be in the record books! The big time colleges are making millions on the successes that a young college student puts forth and the only thing that the students must make certain that they receive in return — is a priceless education!

COLLEGE

Running: Laps — 12, an eqiuvalant of
3 miles

Diet: Official training camp; 3-meals, Steaks,
Fish, Chicken, Green Beans, Vitamins,
Protein Drinks, Sandwiches, Fruit,
Bananas, Milk, Orange Juice, Apple
Juice, Beans, Hot Dogs, Potatoes,
Tangarines, Chicken, Biscuits,
Cole Slaw

Drills: Back-ups, Redirects, Back peddling,
Side-to-Side, 20-sixty yards sprints,
Buzz to the Flats

**Weight
Training:** Monday, Wednesday & Friday Weight
Training Days: 3 sets of 15 reps., Curls,
Bench Presses, Overhead Presses,
Various Chest and "Lat" Exercises,
Leg Extensions, Squats, Indines,
Leg Curls.

additional workout pre-school & just before bedtime

JOE'S TIPS ON TRAINING & DIET

THE POLITICS OF
COLLEGE BALL!

The Politics of College Ball!

I know many people who attended black colleges like Morehouse University or even a school that is not made up of all black students such as, U.S.C., University of Southern California, and they say once a Trojan, always a Trojan. This means that they will take care of their own! The players on the West Coast did not have to endure a lot of the racial criticism and ridicule that we as blacks here in the south had to endure. U.S.C. tends to look after its people long after they have graduated from the school. I feel that this is an area that the Georgia Institute of Technology needs to focus on.

The university should give its students and players more incentive to study hard and it will probably help to boost up the amount of enrolled students at the school! This is one of the downfalls that I experienced. But I didn't know this at the time when I chose the Georgia Institute of Technology as the University of my dreams. The Georgia Institute of Technology is very weak in this area. *But we are working it out for our future players.*

There were many great black athletes that attended while I had the honor of going there. Let's see, there were Greg Horn, Eddie McShan, Eddie Ivory, David Sims, Ruby Allen, Lucius Sanford, Cleo Johnson, Peewee Barnes , and Don Bessillieu.

This was before anybody knew that there were any blacks that attended. Remember, we were covered, by our helmets on the football field. We were the ones that started the "fight" at Georgia Institute of Technology! We were the one's that got the ball rolling for all of the athletes of today.

I must say that I am proud to have set a path for the brothers of today so that they won't have to go through the struggles that I had to go through as a young black athlete in a white man's world!

The average regular student SAT score is 1200, whereas, an athletes score is only *850* on the SAT back then. This is a large gap when you are talking about academic preparation. There were many leaps and bounds in catching up with the academic rigors and social mores of Georgia Technical Institute! There are different situations and challenges that a normal financially deprived or blessed student had to go through. More than just finances, going from the hood of North Carolina to a 99% all white college had a great affects on me. The speech, personal demeanor, dialect — everything was subject for approval.

A Real Friend!

I remember this one new great friend named Beau Bruce, he always wanted to help me out socially and he was instrumental in my cross-cultural growth. He afforded me to go with him to the Kentucky Derby each year. This was an enormous event! We had a great time there and he explained everything to me as best he could without putting me down. The Kentucky Derby was quite a different culture for a black man and I *was game* to pick it up! I owe Beau a lot because it was a foundation for me to see other lifestyles.

Beau was in fact also instrumental in me seeing, Led Zeppelin at the Atlanta Fulton County Stadium. That was truly outrageous. It was when I first was introduced up-front and personally to Rock music and I really understood how much fun white boys had when they partied. These things in the long run made a difference in my overall lifestyle. I was blessed to have friends like Bo. I learned for the most part, as they say, "people, are people, are people, are people" we are really, all the same. There are good people and bad. Everyone has the heart to share ideas about lifestyles but few have the courage to take you where they really live. I have had a lot of exposure over the years to the different cultures and dialects in and out of the United States of America, and it has made me aware of the world outside of the one that I grew-up in and all the different human conditions.

Mother and Father

Family

Son

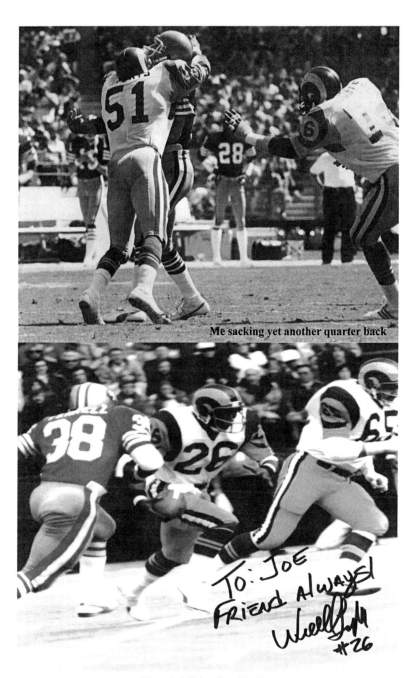

Me sacking yet another quarter back

To: Joe
Friend Always!
Wendell Tyler
#26

Wendell Tyler Rookie Year

Wendell Tyler

1981 LOS ANGELES RAMS

1977 WASHINGTON REDSKINS

GEORGIA TECH'S 1971 FRESHMAN FOOTBALL TEAM

Front Row (Left to Right): Dave Lamb, Mel Rummel, Bob Necessary, Curt Bazemore, Randy Rhino, Jim Robinson, Eddie Ellerbee, Billy Peek, John Abernathy, Steve Whelan, Buster Smith, Jim Voglin.

Second Row: Wayne Hinson, Joby Leahy, Jim Pollock, Rick Hill, William Meeks, Allen Russell, Doug Cooksey, Mike Mercer, Kenny Hallman, Louis Fleming, John Tucci, Frank Schwahn, Steve Dripps, Billy Foy, Bob Tattitch, Barry Lucas.

Third Row: Billy Shields, Gary Jaynes, Bill McLeod, Gary Virene, Joe Harris, Robert McCaskill, Bob Hughes, Jimmy Whittle, Beau Bruce, Frank Fusco, Dave Robinson, Charles Goss, Richard Smith.

Fourth Row: Tom Rassau, Sandy Estill, Mark Bond, Dan O'Donnell, Jim Johnson, Buddy Key, Don Shank, Mike Everson, Stephen Daniel, John Sargent, Bill Powell, John Harchar, Virgil Kilgroe.

MORE ABOUT GEORGIA TECHNOLOGY

More about Georgia Technology

The Georgia Institute of Technology was and is an excellent educational institution. I am able to use my Business Degree and training from Tech to make my living today because I also was a student at *an outstanding educational institution.* Getting a good education gave students at Tech something to fall-back on when and if our talents on the football field gave way.

The professors that taught at the Georgia Institute of Technology when I attended were some of the best in the country. My favorite professor throughout my four years at Georgia Institute of Technology was Professor Long. He was one of my most loyal fans, *a football enthusiast!* Maybe that's why we clicked and hit it off so well. The academic challenges that I had were significant enough; it was a hard school and very serious about its students getting into their books. I struggled many nights studying and praying to pass my exams.

I can even remember sleeping at the library on numerous occasions *just to make the grade.* I remember going without a meal because I knew that if I were to get up from my studies that it would be too hard to pick-up where I had left off.

Please understand that if I didn't *make the grade* I couldn't play and Joseph Alexander Harris had to make it too the football field. I was determined to study; determined to stay on the field because it would bring me much closer to my ultimate goal in life, the N.F.L.! It wasn't just studying, but I had to read, read, read and to retain all of the information that was presented. <u>It was not until twenty years later I found out that I am dyslexic and this helped me to understand why I had to study extra hard.</u> To be able to keep a 2.6 grade point average at a place like Georgia Institute of Technology was an awesome accomplishment for me. To be able to play on this football team you need to keep a 2.0 average. I was one of the blessed ones. My most profound and outstanding achievements while I was at the Georgia Institute of Technology was, that I became the very first black football captain for the Georgia Tech Yellow Jackets team! Impressive? Well, I really am a Yellow Jacket and at Georgia Tech you really had to earn what you got.

I always wanted to also be a leader. I had, I think a lot of potential and Georgia Tech did a darn good job of providing me with "the power of positive thinking". the Georgia Institute of Technology made me a "critical thinker" beyond racial excuses or racial constraints. I have always felt that, " if the system did whatever was needed to get what it expected out of a player — then a player should do the same thing, and get all that he/she can out of the system!".

That's why if you are given the opportunity to get a good education: make the most of it. Get all that you can get! That's what I did. I got all of the education that I could.

Make The Most With Your Team – No Matter The Conditions!

The team that you work on is the only major system to focus on. In sports there are final winners and loser, there is only quality teamwork and individual performances. I loved my Tech teammates and how we struggled to stretch ourselves to new limits just so we didn't let one another down. Once we played against Florida State University and I will never forget that one of their players stated, "I see ya'll have a nigger boy on the team!" He started laughing while one of my main man, Beau Bruce said, "what did he say to you, Joe?" I said, "don't worry about it Bruce, I got this!" Well by then the whole team was upset. That very next play of the game, I will never forget that the player who called me a "nigger" broke through the line and I knocked the "holy heck" out of him and he lay there on his back with the wind knocked out of him!

I stood over him and said, "this is that nigger boy that you are looking up at, how do you like my style?" Now you remember that when they carry you off the field!" Everybody laughed and cheered, "Way to go Joe!" We were a "team" and that's something very hard to explain to people if they have never made firm and lasting commitments to other people. Knowing the guys respected me and would defend my integrity was the greatest single lesson that I ever learned personally and racially.

I had a lot of help during my college years. Maxie Baughn, my linebacker coach taught me an awful lot during those four years. I am grateful to have had the opportunity to study under him. He was a professional linebacker in his time and eventually came on as the linebacker coach. He helped to make me take my talents to the next level.

The Georgia Institute of Technology was known for having some of the best linebackers in the country and I was proud to be one of them. I felt that I was needed while on the team. That is a priceless feeling and opportunity. It is also a precious responsibility. They depended on me to make that big play and to stop the opposing linemen and I must say that I did my job pretty well! This naturally put a heavy load on my shoulders, especially a young man from the hood; but it was something that I really wanted too. I wanted to be the very best of the best and I had encouragement! I had always sought out to be needed and on the team, I felt needed!

Finding and earning your place in life and then performing consistently enough for others to depend on you and to trust that they can need you is why we are alive, I think. One other thing that I learned from attending the Tech was "how-to recognize differences; and understanding which differences make — winners and what distinguishes a loser." Winners, win with critical thinking and a larger perspective about life. They win their 'war games' on the field with what society calls "class"! They have the collective understanding that other people do observe the thinking, action and emotional intelligence of a team. "Classy is as Classy does."

Winners I feel, put God first and then families, school and team next. Winners usually organize a game-plan and agenda for long-term success. They have habits of mind and mental models that help them to focus on successful designs for their lives. They try to do all of the right things in life. These are qualities that make winners stay on top.

Losers on the other hand, lose games and perspective of who they are. They have no grounding or long-term patience or discipline or ideas. They are like fire crackers making one big bang and then they are done forever. They don't last to *represent* in schools, practice, teams, fans, families and society. They have short memories of what's important. They have no style or finesse! They lose without pride or dignity which instigates negative forces in their lives. These forces promote excessive anger, drinking and other escape measures. But when one loses with the pride and dignity of a "good sport," they too are considered winners because tomorrow is another day!

I had to learn from great athletes how-to be a good loser and how-to become a good winner! These are the most important things that I learned while attending the Georgia Institute of Technology! Historically, Georgia Institute of Technology had its fair share of race and economic class oriented obstacles. I had made up my mind that Joe Harris was going to be somebody. The situations that I encountered on campus then helped me to make it in many other political situations. It was hard to maintain that "C+" grade point average and it was even harder to keep up the image on that football field. But determination, friends, teammates and lots of hard work kept me going.

Today, I am an inductee into the Georgia Institute of Technology Hall of Fame and I am proud of the historic teams that I served on. I still hold records that have not been broken! Moral to the story…In your personal future you must stay strong and focused at all times, no matter what circumstances and obstacles may come your way! During the time that I played, I played three years on the main team and one year on the freshman team. No one has come close to becoming the "Jolting Joe". I hit hard; was quick on my feet even as a linebacker and I scored several touchdowns throughout my years at Tech!

I learned at Georgia Tech to become even more of a "gentleman" than my parents taught me to be and that provided me with more opportunities than the average player might have imagined. I must say that I was truly blessed to have the physical abilities that I was born with and was blessed to have the courage to strive for the goals that I had set for myself. Tech made me successful long before I experienced the NFL.

Time flew by and my career exploded into something that I didn't really know how to handle! It all happened so suddenly, four years, great plays, hard hits, and good grades — and "living the life of Riley." I had to ask myself, "What happened?" I'm not complaining by any means, but it makes one wonder, how time really works?

You have to live each and every day as though it is intended and to the utmost! Put all that you have into whatever it is that you set out to do. Make the best of everything that you place your hands on, or make the very best at whatever it is that you are blessed to be a part of.

Yeah, I was part of something that supported me because I made something happen on the field that excited fans of the school to stay vested in all of its activities. Most people don't know what football ticket sales bring to the coffers of universities. It was for me the little things in life that really counted, whether it was a couple of bucks or a couple of hundred bucks. It really meant a lot to me because I was poor! The school kept me going and my mom and dad would send me whatever they had to spare. Twenty-five or thirty dollars wasn't a lot but back then, one was grateful to receive it.

On the weekend, the dining room was closed and we needed that extra cash to get food! I was grateful for any little bit of money that came my way. My older brother and sister would send me five; maybe ten dollars to try to help out my mom and my thanks go out to them, even to this day! The Varsity, a restaurant known for its wonderful hamburgers was one of the places that we spent a lot of time at on the weekends!

Occasionally, I will go by there just to get one of their naked steaks or one of their naked dogs. That was simply a hamburger or a hot dog! Those were a couple of my favorites! I was lucky to have had the skills to be fortunate enough to be accommodated by the Georgia Institute of Technology Athletic Association. Again, that's what great skills, hard work and a lot of determination will do for you!

THE DRAFT

The Draft

One quarter before graduation from Georgia Institute of Technology, I was selected along with 100 other athletes for the possibility to be drafted into the N.F.L. If a college gets four players to become part of the draft then that school did great for any particular year. Most colleges are profoundly lucky to get one or two players that might get drafted into the National Football League.

Not that the luck falls on the school, but the luck and blessings are placed on the draftee. The school just adds another notch into its belt. It gives them a chance to say, hey, in 2004 we had four draftees or three draftees. That is just an example.

When the scouts are looking for their draftees, they are very demanding and tough on you, even arrogant. They want to know if you have the capacity to be *at their beck and call at any given time*. They want to see just how much you hunger to be an N.F.L. player. They will come to your school and at any given time, ask you to do something out of the ordinary.

You can be sitting in class and they will come to get you out of class to, say for instance, and run the 40-yard dash. It could be in the middle of Final Exams! This is around the beginning of April each year.

The draft usually falls at the end of April. What really bothers me is the fact that all year long, the scouts have watched all of the college players at the games and on films and they wait until the time that you are most vulnerable, exam time, and they come and they judge you.

Players didn't know back then if he was even on the potential list of being a "draft pick". It was big-time suspense and even the luck of the draw, so to speak. You didn't know if you were going to be drafted — but the coaches already knew. It was like an initiation. They have "Pro Day" set aside for all college campuses. This is a day when all scouts come to visit your college and take an overall look at particular players. But when I was in college, they just showed up on campus and interrupted your whole day!

Now, they also have a program called a "Combine". Each player is taken to Indianapolis and is tested, mentally and physically to see if they are N.F.L. material. If they pass all of the tests that are given by the N.F.L. then and only then are you eligible to become a professional player.

It doesn't seem fair that the N.F.L. can watch you play all year long on tapes and at the games and then when it comes down to Pro Day and The Combine, they judge you for your performance throughout your career.

One wouldn't think that you could measure professional standards just from one or two days. If a particular player is having a bad day on Pro Day and during The Combine, then, they are passed right on over! It is an extremely stressful period for all players who are possibly nominated as a draftee. This is when a player gets the chance to see the real deal of what makes up the National Football League!

Just think, if you are a 40-yard dash runner and you are a linebacker, if your average run is 4.5, then you're quick! But say for example on Pro Day, you are sluggish and aren't really up to your best, then the N.F.L. has to option to say, "Oh, he isn't the type of material that we need on our team!"

You are judged from one simple performance, even though you have performed well the entire season or four years in college. This will affect many young men and the dreams that they have. Just one bad day and they could lose their dream just that quick, one performance. Look at all of the years of hard work and agony that a player must endure to attain the status of possibly becoming a pro football player.

You could be the one player that ran *25* touchdowns in on season and still judged from one performance. I feel that it is highly unfair to be judge in this manner.

I feel personally that there should be different rules and regulations that a scout should be forced to follow. But this is their way of gaining total control over a person. The ultimate goal is for a player to "be on task and at their total disposal to complete a job".

Many days before the draft, I had hoped and prayed that I would be drafted that year. On the day of the draft, I was 'chilling' with my girlfriend, Mary Beard at her apartment, just relaxing. I didn't watch the draft on television that year because I was so wound up and geared up on the thought that my entire future depended on the outcome of that day's draft. The day that I had longed for and promised my mother that I would become a pro player, all rested on the final outcome of that day!

The next day, I went to school and one of my coaches said that the National Football League had called. He said that they wanted to know the exact phone number to where "Joe Harris" would be on the day of the draft! That was one of the most exciting days of my life! Coach Ken Blair told me that I had gotten a call from the Chicago Bears and that I was drafted in the 7th round! Back then, there were 17 rounds.

But today, there are 7 rounds. With a total explosion, I shouted and jumped with joy! I wanted to see this day all of my life. But more importantly, I prayed that my mother would live to see me be in a true professional football uniform! Don't get me wrong, just to be drafted, doesn't mean that you are a professional football player yet. There are still many trials and tests that a person must endure before being eligible to walk out on the field for a professional team!

Back then, there were 17 rounds in the draft and when I found out that I was drafted in the seventh round, I didn't feel too bad with the numbers. Plus, I was drafted with one of the most outstanding athletes of all time — Walter "Sweetness" Payton. I was honored to be eligible to be on the same team with him. He is now in the National Football League Hall of Fame, along with many other wonderful legends!

Once you are drafted, you still have to make the cut. After it is decided that you have made the team, then you are into negotiating your contract bonuses etc. At the time when I was drafted, the signing bonus were, $6,500.00. That was a lot of money...then. Today the average signing bonus is $350,000.00. My story is that of a 7th round pick. But if you are good enough to become one of the first or second round picks today, the signing bonus is far into the millions of dollars!

Advice...

When negotiating a contract, it is good to have an agent. But back when I was drafted, it really wasn't enough money to have an agent.

Just because a person lands a contract after he or she has been drafted, doesn't mean that they are set in stone. There is still a long road ahead in order that you might hold onto that position with that team. There is the great possibility that if a player doesn't play in the first six games then that player is subject to not getting the things that were promised in the contract that was signed by all participating parties.

Let's say that a player does make it to the sixth game and after that, he doesn't play anymore. Then that player is only eligible to receive half of what was stated in his contract and not all contracts are the same. Each contract differs from one to the next and depending on the contract players can and will be subject to getting cut any time during the first few games in his contractual career.

The contract is a legal agreement that the N.F.L. designs to cover itself as an organization   if you do not perform to their standards. Please, if you have made it to the point of negotiating a contract with the National Football League then please, please, invest in an attorney so that he or she may review your contract and all of the fine print that it entails.

At this point you must also please...pray to Our Father in Heaven that you succeed in finishing out a season without injury! If a player is injured in the first or second game of the season then depending on their contract The National Football League has the option to tear up the contract.

That basically sums up what a draft really is about. Of course there are more technical aspects of becoming a draftee for the National Football League. But, I'm certain that if you have made it to that point in your career, then you are sure to find out that all that is presented to you may not be all that good for you.

I remember the day that I found out that I had been drafted very vividly! I was so happy. So happy by the fact that my mother who was somewhat ill at the time was able to witness that I had succeeded in reaching my dream of becoming a National Football League player. I was so happy when the coach told me that Chicago had called me.

When I returned the call, it was explained that they wanted to discuss my future with whoever was handling it. I told them that my coach, Maxie Baughn and I would supply them with all of the necessary information. I didn't feel that I needed an agent, although I had a few that were contracted, so Coach Baughn and I negotiated the final contract.

They explained that the phone call was just a welcoming call to inform me that I had been elected as one of the lucky players to have been drafted by the Chicago Bears. They went on to tell me that I was to fly up to Lake Forest, Illinois for a small mini-introductory camp hosted by the Bears. I couldn't wait to get there. I counted each passing moment with shear anticipation! Almost everyone around me was just as excited as I was. I had become one of the people to go down into the history books by having my name placed as one of America's *1974-75* National Football League Draft!

My jersey number with the Chicago Bears was *"50"*. I was so proud to wear that jersey. I was always number 50, 51, and 52 and once in Canada, I was number 45. They said that I was so quick on my feet that I fit into the running back series of numbers.

I have to give honor to God that I was able to sustain the contract that I signed in the beginning and live to play in more than just the six-game spread, but I was blessed enough to play for over ten years with the N.F.L. even though I was back and forth, from the Canadian League to the National Football League. They were still all professional leagues.

THE NATIONAL FOOTBALL LEAGUE

The National Football League

It was an extraordinary honor to play as a champion in the National Football League (NFL). It is great that people will be able to go to www.google.com and see that Joseph A. Harris is really associated with American Football. Being a part of the N.F.L. is a personal management and business opportunity, and not a luxury! The N.F.L. is a profound system to be a part of. National attention, ideas of celebrity and prefabricated expectations for one's celebrity status — must be managed correctly by the new professionals so that they ultimately make the most of the N.F.L. benefits. There is an old saying, "what is good to you may not be good for you in the long run."

I want you to stay with me on this point, because it may become somewhat confusing to some of you though it may be self-explanatory to others. I would like to start this chapter off by telling you a few of the stories that I experienced while I was in the National Football League.

Disclaimer: But first, I would like to explain that these are my experiences and they should not in any way have any reflection on the others who have been or are a part of the Nation Football League. I repeat that it these are my thoughts, opinions and experiences. When a football player moves through the ranks of playing college ball to playing pro ball, there are many different situations and emotions that come into play.

Here are some of my observation about some of the attitudes and questions entertained in that transition:

1) First of all, during tryouts, in the very beginning, a player is blessed to experience the feeling of playing with the best football players in the world and with that comes, mixed emotions.

2) Some of those emotions are: am I good enough? Can I be the person that I'm expected to be? Will I be one of the many that will go through the misfortune of being cut from the team?

3) Can I make an impact on the veteran football players that had made up that team in the years before me?

4) Will the players and coaches like me as a person in general?

   Asking this makes you realize that you are up against a historic legacy regarding the position that you play on a team and many people have come and gone, after playing with the team in the position that you play. You occupy a *spot in the industry* that will be there with or without you for many, many years. One must face the fact that they are expendable. Needless to say after that one starts to understand that there can only be so many stars. Everyone keeps in mind that it is all about talent, performance and politics. Still other questions are:

6) Will I be able to manage my salary to the best of my ability in a way that will be in the best interest of me and my family?

7) Do I have all of the necessary team players in my personal life to help me stay focused and to aid in guiding me towards making the right investments throughout my professional football career?

8) Will my career be as promising financially beyond the realms that my contract states in the distant future?

9) Will I end up failing as a man by turning to drugs and alcohol like the media sometimes reports? (The media searches and seeks for professional athletes when they fall down. And they feed on things of that nature to capitalize on a top story.)

10) Can I survive the season without injury?

11) Will I be able to withstand the physical trauma that I'm about to embark upon?

12) Can I live up to the expectation of the fans that support our team?

13) Is the National Football League all that it is cracked up to be by the media and society as a whole?

I can answer the last question with a big NO! The media and society leads us to believe that the National Football League is full of glamour and riches but that is very far from the truth! The league only pays the big bucks to a select hand full of players that tend to make up the majority of plays that it takes to win a game. These are the players that make the headlines and bring in the revenue to pay the salaries of the players on the team, the coaches and the people that make up the entire N.F.L corporate force.

To sum it all up, a player goes through some major emotional trauma, much like the physical trauma that he or she has endured through their high school and college years, which is the same trauma that has brought them to this point in their career. After I was drafted and I made all of the necessary cuts in order to officially be considered as one of the Chicago Bears, I was elated! I could "out-shine the sun in the sky!" I had worked hard enough to fulfill my dreams and all of its requirements.

Today unlike many of the players that you see on television I have developed a life beyond the playing years and the game itself. And though I still love the game and my opportunities, I am hoping to create better conditions for all athletes that play in the NFL. I want to tell my story of what the National Football League is really all about! Again, I must express the fact that these are my opinions, thoughts and experiences and they should in no way reflect others who have been a part of or are presently affiliated with the National Football League.

After signing my contract, I played with the Chicago Bears for only part of one seasonal year. After all, the amount that an older N.F.L. retired player's pension isn't as glamorous as the players that you see or the newly retired players' pensions. The media only tells society half of the story and most of it is "misleading". This is where having a good education comes is a lifesaver and great insurance.

The NFL pay scales when I was involved had small increments and certainly were not what fans and the rest of the public would even believe. Athletes were some times taken advantage of by the industry, the athlete compromises just to stay on board. I have seen guys sometimes compromise a lot just to stay on teams just to be on TV. A few to me seemed like they almost played in the league for free.

In the beginning of athletic careers, people are elated just being professional and they tend to overlook the fine details of the contracts that control their careers. If they haven't been steadfast financially, when they reach retirement they could have very little financial resources to fall back on. Did you know, for example a professional basketball player's pension plan is a lot different from that of a professional football player's. Major League Baseball allows retired players to participate in its long-term contracts cost-of-living increases, but the N.F.L. does not. I think that we should have some equity in the sustained popularity of the industry.

The N.F.L.'s pension is just what it was at the beginning of the original contract. Retired athletes are lead by a National Football League Union supervisor. His job is to keep things afloat for those like myself who have made it to the retirement stage in the professional world of football.

The late, Gene Upshaw a former offensive lineman for the Oakland Raiders held the position. Mr. Upshaw had to protect the contracts of the active players and the retired players. Today Atty. DeMaurice Smith is the new executive director of the NFL Players' Association (www.nflplayers.com). We are very excited about Atty. Smith and his formidable ties to U.S. Atty. General Eric Holder and the Obama administration. The retired players were very concerned about equity and their futures because once a player reached the point of retirement it is totally out of the players' hands to negotiate settlements. It is the leadership of the supervisor of the Union that will determine the financial futures of many of former stars that you have grown to love who played our nation's beloved game.

The NFL as a business has grown a lot improved over the years and older players believe that they contributed to the branding and popularity. One would think that a little consideration for those who contributed to the National Football League would have benefits on the scale of its enormous growth.

The National Football League is one of the top corporate associations in the United States averaging hundreds of millions of dollars each successive year because of the efforts of players like as myself who worked really hard for increased fan entertainment, team and league accomplishments. I personally think that the industry should be willing and capable of sharing the wealth, for what that is worth. The, "what have you done for us lately" is a sad sentiment and sense of respect to approach retired champions with. In other words, they tend to have forgotten who made the N.F.L. the season by season success that it is today.

The year that I was drafted, a Coach by the name of Jack Pardee out of the United States Football League, the Birmingham Stallions, had just landed the position of head coach for the Chicago Bears. I was honored and happy to become a Chicago Bear with Jack leading the team. I was sure that we were out to win the Super Bowl that year, but as you well know, a player may or may not stay with the team of his choice. It is the luck of the draw when it comes down to the N. F. L assignments.

A linebacker by the name of Eddie Sheeks and I had the opportunity to work out together and to study the defensive linebacker strategies during the summer after college. Eddie was a good friend of Jack Pardee and so I kind of had the inside scoop. He was aware of the defense that Jack liked and he and I took it to heart. I was a rookie and had the distinct pleasure of working out and learning plays from a professional football player during the summer. This made me stand out above the rest.

Jack Pardee was the coach of a World League team located in Alabama. He was selected as the head coach of the Chicago Bears. Both Eddie and I were selected to play for the Chicago Bears and selected to go with the new coach. Eddie had tremendous skills as a linebacker. Again, I guess politics came into play, because although I was a great football player and there were many others like me. It is "who you know" and not always "what you know" that can get you ahead in the game. You can be the best guy and not even make it. So don't be discouraged just stay in school and get educated.

I'll never forget it, Eddie had a Lincoln Continental and he had a tarp that he covered the car with that read "Fast Eddie" painted on it. Eddie lived in the east portion of Atlanta, near Murphy High School, and it seemed that he and I were a sure thing. I was so elated to spend that summer working along side of a wonderful player like "Fast Eddie".

Eddie and I would go the college athletic department and we would work out doing squats, pull downs, bench presses and lots of a jogging. We would do five-mile runs on a golf course that had lots of hills. This helped our endurance and stamina to reach new heights. Mostly we did our workout with the weights. I recall learning a tremendous amount of skills which stuck with me all of the days of my life.

Eddie was very familiar with the tactics of Jack Pardee and what he expected from athletes. So Eddie and I focused on all of the things that would make Jack notice us. This prepared me for the practices that would eventually make me stand out like a prize and I gained a lot of recognition from Jack as a coach.

Those days really had a profound effect on my memories and they stand-out as starting points in my professional football career. And it was great football generals (coaches) and players like those guys that made a significant influence on me to become one of the players that would go down in history and have a "household name" in my era and a name that you can 'Google' today having contributed to American Football.

TO BE BLACKBALLED

To Be Blackballed

Being blackballed means that, "you have messed-up so bad" that "no team wants to touch you". You are for-all-intent-and-purpose, thrown or "*to be cast into the sea,* so to speak *with no way to get ashore*". It means that you are placed on a list that is somewhere out there and if your name is on it, you are, just what is says, Black-balled!

My best advice to high school students is to "keep your nose clean"! Stay out of trouble. Practicing these measures will start you on the right track so that once you enter college you will have studied and learned from the previous players who were black balled for various reasons. This will enable you to not follow into their footsteps and stay on the right path.

Start out early and "*do the right thing*". This not only applies to athletes, but it applies to all aspects of owning your own "commonsense"!

Each and every one of us knows what is right and what is wrong. Stay clear from those negative forces and practice being a good judge of character. Simply, know the people that you hang around.

You may not do anything directly, but, suppose you are with a couple of guys and they just happen to decide to rob a bank or hold up a store, there goes your reputation, freedom and career!

Sometimes, we must weed out our gardens so that new flowers can bloom. Think, about that! It may sound to you like being placed on a simple list won't stop you from succeeding if you are an outstanding player, but, what I am telling you is... "if one is put on a black-ball list it can certainly be the end of one's career!"

MY ADVICE TO DREAMERS

My Advice to Dreamers

When I became a professional football player, I had the privilege of being "backup" to the great Chris Hamburger! He played for the Washington Red Skins. I remember thinking how proud I was just to be on the same field as him. It's a heck of a thing to one day meet some of the same people whom I idolized as a child. Many kids only dream the dreams, but I was fortunate enough to live out the dreams that I had as a child.

When I was twelve years old, I remember telling my mom that someday, I would be a pro football player and play in the Super Bowl. I fantasized growing up and moved out to California to pursue my dreams. Try to remember that, "if you believe, if you never give up, it all happens". Even as a child, I had full confidence in myself. I never 'sold myself short' or "bowed-down" to the level of those who were jealous of me. "Believe you me", during my lifetime, I've met my share of several envious and mean spirited people who would like nothing more than to see me fail.

During your lifetime, you must enjoy whatever you do. The whole key to expect success, expect joy and expect fulfillment – and that's what you'll receive. This mind-set alone is success! Go about everyday life disassociating yourself with any negativity. I remember my grandfather telling me that I should never speak "things" into existence. I couldn't fully comprehend this as a kid, but now I understand and appreciate those powerful words. "Thank you Granddaddy". He has long since passed, but he will live forever in my memories. Never let go of your dreams and put your focus on a goal and strive to reach it, letting nothing stand in your way.

Developing the power of positive thinking is an awesome challenge for anyone to undertake and to achieve. It takes a kind of daily and consistent discipline and power that helps you to shape what you learn from life each day in order to create new realities. Positive thinking makes you an upbeat person with an attitude people like to have around on and off the field. I believe that God gives us powers. I believe that he helps us to evolve into better human beings and when we apply positive thinking, it automatically makes us better individuals. If we spread to others the 'force' of positive thinking then we sowed new seeds for "light" to grow around us!

I have always had this strange feeling that people absorb one another's' energy. We absorb attitudes and perspectives that are both positive and negative. I made one of my missions to try to be a positive influence and an asset to the people that I know and meet. Doing this, makes for a positive career, both mentally and physically. Negative influences are not good for health, careers or for business. Negative influences pull you down in ways that you aren't aware. Stay away from negative people. I have an old saying and it goes like this: "weed-out your garden so that your flowers can bloom." Think about it!

Getting caught up with negative people may cause you to loose your glory. In other words, they can steal your glory! A person's negative "attitude" towards life can and will rub off on you. Before long, you will begin to have a negative attitude just like them. We can't always choose the people that we work with, or have to deal with on a daily basis. Therefore, you must stay focused. Keep a positive outlook on everything that you are involved with. Don't let others steal your glory.

"Staying focused" doesn't mean that you have to totally abandon the negative crowd. This simply means that you should try spreading a little 'positive spirit' on them when you can. This is called in the eyes of the Lord, "sowing seeds". You will reap harvest from it someday! Jealous people definitely have a negative outlook on life. That's why it is best that you steer clear of the people who don't want you to succeed. There again, stealing your glory!

If stealing your glory makes them happy they are not interested in your best interest. They are jealous because they may not be as good at one thing or another or they may not know how to socialize productively. They may not know how to share a good word and forward-moving successes.

If you notice, most jealous people either stick close to other jealous people or they are alone most of the time. That's because no one wants to be around people like that.

Most lonely people are miserable. They bring this on themselves because of their negative attitudes and it's kind of goes in a vicious circle. There are many obstacles that can come in the way of one's success. There are more than just negative people; there can be negative places too. Negative places are where you already know 'within' that you can count on trouble. There simply isn't a good way to explain why and where you should be. I can only suggest that you use your commonsense and keep your goals in the forefront of your mind at all times. Thinking about your goals can really help to keep you focused. By doing this, it can bring you that much closer to becoming successful.

Often people treat one another the way that they are treated themselves. This has a lot to do with the way that they were reared.

The way that you are brought up has an awful lot to do with your attitude as an adult. Living a "negative lifestyle" today doesn't have to be so because you grew up in a negative environment. You don't have to claim vicious cycles like they are "generational curses". I believe that you can protect your own life through positive thinking and good decisions. You must pray it away. You have to 'work it away 'from you and the life that you hold dear.

Sometimes we have to fight to stay away from these negative forces. It isn't easy at times, but you should spread positive feedback to cushion the blow while you destroy weeds from the garden. Understand that there is a tough road that you must travel in order to make the dreams that you dream come true, so, be prepared to work hard at creating positive and supportive relationships and environments.

You have to grow physically and mentally to improve character. Find joy and fulfillment in whatever you dream. Remember, dreams do come true, and I am living proof. Be confident in yourself. You can and will manage the stages of growth and development to become a successful athlete and a successful person.

Remember that the price for success is quite expensive. Be prepared to pay whatever the cost may be, while keeping your dignity and self-respect. You must understand from the very beginning, each and every one of you, who wish to become professional athletes, need to start good behavioral habits or patterns that you live by, act on and that go 'into practice' each and every day of your life. Living right takes discipline and hard work.

EXPECTATIONS

Expectations

I mentioned earlier that football players were, in many ways considered special individuals. They are given special privileges and are sometimes expected to always do things in bigger ways than the average guys or 'larger than life". Football is a game of pushing grown men around and taking down guys in the very best of physical shape. One has to out think an opponent, out run and out maneuver all in-your-face opposition.

I think that perhaps even throughout the history of football, the player's were unconsciously prepared to live by an ever changing set of rules and prepared a readiness for a lifestyle of bold and abrasive exchanges.

I believe that the mind-sets of professional football athletes are shaped by and perpetuated by coaches, managers, adoring fans, the stand-out players and the "Big-Man culture" that preceded us. I believe that this can be a form of inherited psychological manipulation if one is not in control of him-self and does not approach the profession with a truly balanced life. The "wild-man" personae of the game of football is outdated. Don't get "brain washed" into thinking that football players are mindless brawn with no academic and business "know-how"!

Only the negative players living up to the old stereotypes and uncaring business-management gets all-the-consequences and repercussions of players who are out of control. We all know men in the N.F.L. who have lost considerable money, good marriages and great reputations playing wild and care-free off the field. The myth of 'untouchable men' in the pro league has directly led to the career failures of many good men. In real life everyone must subscribe to laws, decency and human politics.

Politics, plays a large role in all sports. Politics plays a role in each and every one of our lives. I think that many people don't realize when they're going through it. I, for one, have dealt with politics on a daily basis almost as far back as I can remember. You see, adults and kids have goals, coaches and athletes have goals; college administrations and coaches have goals, ticket box offices and fans have goals, and "stars" and "father time" have needs, realities and goals. Can you see the picture that I am trying to paint?

For as long as I can remember playing the game, we were taught that we were "above the average". We were to be tough and to take nothing that 'anyone' had to offer that we didn't want. Each player has to interpret for himself and personalize what "tough" and what "larger than life" is against men and those who would develop opposition to them in life. Each player must learn what toughness they will exhibit even with women and children off of the field and out of the way of the cameras. And what toughness and larger than life means when people want help themselves to shares of the fruits or the privileges of the player's hard-won labors.

Naturally, we were treated special by all kinds of people and we are expected to be always tough "like a brick wall". Everyone seems to have expectation about your personae as a pro player. Coaches, fans and communities that we represented instilled into football players that: "nothing should be able to stand in the way of a true winner". You must be like a brick wall, you are not penetrable". "You must be able to take a body punch from a steel ball. You are hard as steel".

Corporately and strategically, it is the duty of a good coach to push athletes to the furthest point that human beings can physically go. They are professional motivation experts. They put in your mind that you can go farther than you ever thought your human body was capable. Sometimes this conditioning makes you think that because you have sacrificed and you are trained and you are dangerous to all opposition that you are entitled to new realms of glory, money and bling, bling! See?

The best coaches help you to train your mind on what is ahead for you on the football field but you may also need a life coach. Not to go on a tangent but remember that a basketball players' stance is important to a football player. I know that, that sounds funny? But it teaches you to condition yourself so you are concerned with "the outcomes". Hard work and dedication makes a good athlete. The coaches drive you to the limit, in all aspects to become a pro.

Part of conditioning is pain. There's no way around it. All the way back, as far as junior high, the football coach's would give us salt tablets if we were cramping. I had a serious problem cramping on the field. They wouldn't give me water they gave us salt tablets instead. This was a terrible thing for me because I hated to take those salt tablets, but pain and endurance makes you stronger in the long run.

You know that while you are enduring that pain, you might think that it is the worst thing in the world. Mind-control is a key ingredient! It is also called "discipline" and the power-of-determining "mind-over-matter" when you are confronting pain. This plays a positive role when you, want a future in sports. Mind-control makes you stronger and able to tolerate the torture that sometimes is placed on you out there on the field. As you know, too much salt causes more cramping. You do the math!

I do think that we are like 21st century gladiators and Olympiads, check out the hype. Look! Like in

Roman times the Olympiad (a person who is champion in the Olympics), is treated and expected to perform above the levels of most average men. "Champions" you see, do not have average appetites for anything. Life is one kind of "game" or another.

Most average men desire to have one woman, a football player of old, were as a matter of stamina and "hearty appetite "expected to play the field and have two or three women. This was not to mention decadent group parties. The media has told the public, that the life of a professional athlete is full of "glitz and glamour" and "fun fatigue". Even today, sure, the money is good, if you are a truly good player! But, they neglect to tell you the whole story. Always keep in mind that "everything has a price" and "someone must pay the cost."

Sometimes the fee is extremely high. Notice that not everyone is as popular as the next guy.

That's why not all contracts are written the same, so people don't expect the unexpected. Being a "team-player" is very important, not only in sports but, in everything that you do, if it involves others. No team will tolerate anything less than you're being strong and positive and sincere about reaching the goal 'that you say' that you desperately desire in the organization.

You must "buckle-down" and condition yourself both mentally and physically.

I'm not writing this book to belittle to anyone else, nor is the purpose of this book to have any negative reflections on the National Football League from a professional point of view. The sole reason that I wrote this book is to tell my story. Writing this was my form of therapy. I needed to express myself in an open manner in order to relieve a lot of built up tension, anxiety from years of growth, travel and hard reflection.

It has been cathartic for me. I finished a whole period of my life and I "exhaled" with the good and the bad. I would also like to get a message to all young people out there who have fantasies of a football career. You should not use rose colored glasses and if you take this journey. I say this with all sincerity and from my heart. Football is the world's greatest club to belong to, but "guard and defend your future like you guard and defend the ball".

FOOTBALL STRATEGIES

Football Strategies

L ife in football is pretty much centered on a coach like I said before. Players learn skill sets of "control" from coaches. Ways to control the weight of men coming at you; ways to eat, run and build muscles and ways hopefully to manage the entire culture. Players must feel confident in themselves, their teams and their "game." Players must feel indestructible.

Attitudinal changes to portray greatness are part of the game and each coach has his own way of motivating his team. Some coaches have a sense of humor and use phrases like, "let's move it girls!" or "ladies get your dress tails out of your butt!"

Almost everyone get's a private nickname on the team. Certain names are called also when you're pushing yourself that make you feel great. Remember that I told in my high school, we were called the "Mighty Five", which was the starting line-up. Naturally all coaches have the ultimate goal to win, but I feel that each sector has a different strategy and other goals.

Every coach that I have known will forever try to get the most out of a player, by any means necessary. They expect that you always give 200%, at practice and more importantly 300% during each game.

Tactically, as I mentioned earlier in this book, I feel that one can coach one's self. Remember I strongly feel that the stance of a basketball player (guard) and his gracefulness was helpful to my progress as a good football player. I played guard when I was into basketball and it is another quality that a cornerback and a linebacker needs in order to be able to cover his target. The coordination that a basketball player needs to be successful is just as important to a football player. He needs the agility and skills to move quickly on his feet while still bouncing the ball.

Football players, instead of bouncing the ball, the coordination takes place when one can do the job that the team requires, (blocking, tackling, or running the ball) and "the entire team" keeps its eyes on the football. Same difference!

Just as on a basketball court, some of the same strategies apply. The games may be different, but the same concept of winning is the main idea. A good athlete in general must be ready-to-learn what's going on.

The good athlete must be rested and alert; must have good vision and good hearing abilities. You must be able to see your opponent with your peripheral vision. You must hear him coming as well — to give you that extra edge and get the upper hand on that player. Brushing up on your eye-hand-coordination and your listening skills will be a plus to your performance.

From a linebacker's point of view, the man who is able to take on two or more blockers will be far more successful than a blocker who can handle only one man. This is really common sense! This was one quality that I possessed.

I had the ability to take and sit down three or more opponents! In addition to the force behind my attack, this made me stand out from many of the other great players who were just as good but didn't have this kind of technique or skill set to manage the behavior of more than one or two men.

This learned skill and technical know-how creates the savvy of a pro ball player. It is the trade of being a good linebacker." I always liked being one on one, man to man and man on man. I would hold onto my target and did whatever it took to take that man down. I had great coverage from all angles on the field. This attribute made me one of the great player's.

From a field level point-of-view there are many things that can make a player better than you. For instance, one player might be faster than you are. One might hit just a little harder than you. All of this should not deter you from learning from your weak areas. Learn the foundations and techniques that these men developed to improve their games.

The great thing about being on a team is that you hopefully can learn from others and contribute individually to a collective "excellence." Those that are strong in certain areas also must have a weak area. I took the opportunity when I played to focus and study the next guy's "form and style of play". This enabled me to become stronger in my weak areas before my weaknesses were even noticed.

It took a lot of trials and errors before I became strong in certain areas. It paid off once I got on the field and went head-on against stronger players. What I'm trying to say is, just because a player might seem to be better than you are, take advantage of his strong points and turn your weak points into strong ones. This not only applies to football, this psychology, readiness and strategic approach — works in all aspect of life. I also learned from many years on the field that investigating a player's family background, personality and strategies on and off the field worked to my advantage also. This aided in my becoming such a success on and off the field.

I already told you that you need to understand exactly what a coach expects from his players. You have to be able to look at things from his perspective and not just from the player's perspective. There are many things to look for. Let's say that a certain coach has 'real problems' with players that "give up" instead of completing assignments on the field. That could make this coach angry and cause verbal outbreaks where he calls you, "less than a friend". To avoid that, I would always put forth 200% effort and this always pleases that particular type of coach. Or if a coach is one, that like's to offer words to build confidence and encouragement, then you would always listen with both ears as well as consume all the materials that he passes out.

Just by having your undivided attention will cause that type of coach to have just a little more respect for you than he may have for a teammate who shrugged him off as being just a pesky old man.

These are all simple, yet they are important common-sense strategies for your success in the sports community. I'm sure that you will learn something everyday if you are ready-to-learn on and off the field from each instance and every situation. I did!

Younger athletes are big and strong. They tend to be stronger and able to outrun the next player. If you are a young player, hard work and focusing on your goals along with these positive attributes will help you develop into becoming a finer athlete. This is not to say that an older pro player is slower or weaker than the younger guy. This just explains what individuality means to an old or young player. A player must want to do what he does. He has to have a burning desire to become an outstanding player. Even if he is good but has no fire and desire, he will not shine like "the Star" that could be deep down inside of him. You have to love the sport and all that comes with it in order to be successful.

If you look at all of the hard work that you are putting into perfecting and protecting your prestigious position on the field then understand that it takes this and a whole lot more to reach the goals that you are setting for yourself. Hard work without 100% of your heart and mind in it means that you are working for nothing.

All of these football strategies can work in your favor. Let's keep in mind that not all athletes will make it to the pros. But if you focus on making your skills the best that you can offer, then being a great high school player will lead you to earning a scholarship to a fine college.

Let's just say that hard work and dedication is economically worthwhile. My older brothers had to work hard to put themselves through college and I know that this had to be awfully hard on them and their families. But thank God they made it and didn't get distracted by all of the temptations that we often see throughout our lifetimes.

Did you know that there are thousands of athletes that don't get the opportunity of getting scholarships? There are those who may be good, but opportunity just passed right by them. I say all of this to make a point, "always expect the worst but pray for the best".

God forbid, a player has an accidental injury in the middle of his college career. He still has to go on without an education to earn a living for himself and family. That's why it is important to always have something to fall back on. Your scholastic abilities are just as important as focusing and working hard at the sport that you pray for success in.

Knowing why you do what you do, whether it's football, basketball, tennis or even chess is very important! I always advise that one realize that no one is forcing you to go out there and do what you do.

Participating in a sport is an elective and not something that is required. Therefore, know the "what and the why" of what you do for your self.

This will also help you to better your skills in the chosen field. "Purpose" has its place in your life. It helps you to communicate and sell your talents and ideas to others who ask you about your future. Knowing exactly what your purpose is also reinforces your own "self-determination."

It has always been said that some athletes have tunnel-vision. This means that they only see straight ahead and their minds and eyes don't actually see what might distract them from the desired success. It also means that a player only concentrates on the sport and nothing else. Not a good idea! Not only in football, but, in all of life's situations, please, always have a balance in your life and a comprehensive backup plan.

Keep in mind, football is not a sport that you can play all of your life. With time, we grow old. As we grow old, our bodies tend to weaken. Our minds are not as sharp and neither are our reflexes. Plus, keep in mind that there are many, many other athletes just waiting to take your place with that team that you are a part of. Take it from me, a country boy from Evans Hills in the heart of the small town called Fayetteville, North Carolina. I know that opportunity can easily pass you right over. I was truly blessed to be given all of the opportunities that I was given.

I was blessed with these things because, I worked hard at the sport and I focused on the goals that I had set when I was a child. I always tried to listen to my elders and I tried awfully hard to do the right things on and off of the field. I suggest that you do the same if your dream is to become a reality. Stay focused and trying to always *do the right thing* in life can get pretty hard at times.

If your EXPECTATIONS are to become a successful professional athlete, then tell yourself, 'Nothing is too hard. Succeeding through the hardships will make me strong!'

ARE YOU READY TO BE A PRO?

Are You Ready to be a Pro?

Iknow that there are hundreds of thousands of people, who wish to become professional athletes, but there is a lot that is required to reach that point. If you look throughout sports history, you will see that all of those who have reached the point of stardom, worked extremely hard. The kind of hard work that requires that each and every waking moment is spent either thinking or practicing or conditioning one's body.

Unless you are one of the luckiest people on earth, born with the skills that will make you "a household name" in professional sports, then you will have to prepare for each and every day of your life by thinking, practicing and conditioning yourself. You will be "doing these things", so that you will stand out and be noticed. There are at least forty-five players that make up a complete football team. And in the professional league, there are only, maybe seven stars that come out of the season.

Five or so players per team will become the top players will probably have enough finances all along to retire on —so ask yourself, what happens to the rest of the players and their futures? Here a sense of the process. In the beginning a player is given a standard contract. A contract that is, healthy enough to purchase a nice house and car. After that large sum is gone, then what? Prior to "being in the game" so to speak. You are just a fan of the pros, like everyone else.

The average fan, doesn't know anything about the "business of the football industry." The N. F. L. is a business like all businesses and it wants to maximize its profits. The public only knows what the media presents via newspapers, television and advertisements. The truth is shaded by a life that is full of "glitz and glamour"!

No one hears what happens to injured players. I mean, say for instance that a player was the star on his college or high school team, (there are some players who are good enough to go straight from high school to the pros), and he or she lands a contract for say, *2.5* million dollars. The lifestyle that a professional athlete needs to live up to, per the media, is extravagant, correct?

Well, most athletes try to live up to the lifestyle that the last or former athlete lived. You know, a large house in the finest of neighborhoods, Mercedes Benz or Hummer, the best of expensive furniture and then, he has to look the part, that is as far as clothes are concerned. As we all know,

Gucci, Dolce Gabana and Evisu, etc. ... are very expensive! Am I correct?

Well, that wraps up well over half the salary, especially when that 'star' as they want to be called, has to pamper and dress and "fix everything" so that his or her spouse is up to par as well, correct? Now...if you live to that extreme, just exactly how long do you think that, the initial, and the little money will last? No longer than a year or two tops! And, let's say that, God forbid, he has an injury that prohibits them from playing for the duration of the season. Where do you think he is headed?

If the N. F. L. as a business organization realizes that they are out of 2.5 million dollars and are left without their "Star". How do you think they will handle that? They have to renegotiate the players' contract. Keep in mind that there are "clauses" that cover the organization "built-in" to cover their losses somewhere in the original contract! You have to protect every asset also too.

Here's some bottom-line information. For the N. F. L. to negotiate a contract means that, "a player has to play in at least six games or the league can, and will simply tear-up the contract!" Further, "If a player does play in at least six games with or without injury then the N. F. L. is required to pay only half of the salary that is stated on that contract."

So…at no given time should a player be complacent about their contract with the National Football League! You must be on top of the demands on you. If the league didn't cover itself, then it would be giving money away. The business itself suggests that there is a "risk" that you the player and "Star" will possible not last through the expensive contract.

If the N. F. L. didn't consider that particular "risk factor" then the organization as a business would have gone bankrupt long, long ago. Let's say that a player is good enough to make the team, but isn't good enough to be the 'star'. Well, that player would naturally receive a contract for a lesser amount of salary.

The game and industry is all about investment, risks, and performance. Everyone risks: players, families, franchises, leagues. These are only a few of the things that a person should be prepared mentally and emotionally for. Prayer does have its place!

Believe you me the physical aspect is far more important! One must be cautious of injuries. This is one of the most important things to consider when one signs a contract. None of us anticipates having an injury, but face it, they do happen. It may not be because of something you did wrong, but because of the laws of gravity. Maybe your body turns wrong or you fall in a difficult manner and break a bone, or fracture one. Maybe you tear a tendon, or whatever may cause one to be sidelined or benched.

These things do happens, even though we hope and pray that they don't. Many of these "risks" are things that are not well thought-out by young people who have dreams of becoming the next "household name" in sports. I might add that a lot of emphasis should also be placed on finding the right person or firm to negotiate your original contract. This firm or person is called an "agent". That alone requires a lot of research, investigation and probing into. To find a good agent, one must, first of all, *find out what is in it for them and why they feel that they can help you.*

Many times, an athlete automatically assumes that, if someone or some firm tells them that *the earth is square* and this sounds good to them. Then that athlete will believe in that firm or person. The athlete then will place his future in the hands of what could possibly be "the devil" literally. One must discretely, search and inquire about the person or firm that he is interested in. Research and investigate the firm or person's professional background and career as a sports agency. You are far better off than we were because today you can "Google" a firm or person.

Once you have found that special agent, then you must find a good attorney to follow behind them. I know this seems like a lot of unnecessary work if that firm or person has all of the right credentials. But, trust me these details must be explored if the player wants, what is in his or her best interest. When choosing someone, also remember, that they will have your entire future in their hands. Please, again take my advice and dig deep into their past. Their past may tell you how much trust (if any) that you can or should place with them. This is really common sense, but a lot of times, we all sometimes tend to "block out the sun to feel the rain", do you understand?

Okay, now, say that a player is one of the featured "five" stars on a team and let's say that he gets a contract for say, a million dollars a year and he of course must "live to the extreme". The "extreme life" of a multi-millionaire will naturally cause him or her to shell out, far more than the average millionaire, am I correct?

Alright, now, let's say that the lifestyle that the media promotes for a person of this financial condition — is so grand — that most people couldn't even think of enough ways to spend it all. The "Star" sometimes ends up believing the hype and promo and not their pockets. They "get the big head" and arrogantly go to the point that they mess up all of their money. Many don't invest any of it. Well you can do the math, what then?

HONOR TO MY COACHES

To Honor My Coaches

E. E. Smith recruited me from Washington Drive and it was on that football team that I played linebacker. This is the beginning of the story about "the legendary Joe Harris", also known as the "Stud" :>).

I really felt honored and proud as a sophomore to play with the varsity high school team as a starter — I enjoyed this immensely. To name a few of our coaches that we had throughout my high school days, there was: Coach Bishop Harris, Coach William Carver, Coach D.T. Carter and Coach Ike Walker.

Coach Bishop Harris was the most motivational coach that I have ever had the pleasure of knowing throughout my entire career. He was the one that always thought that a football player should have more than one of everything.!"

Coach William "Bill" Carver was the man who taught me to be challenging. He would put the five toughest guys on the front line. We were called the "Mighty Five"! Coach D.T. Carter was a man of medium height, bald headed and mean as a hornet! He was somewhat called, 'the brains of the operation' for the "Mighty Golden Bulls" at E. E. Smith High School. He was the best at putting together an offensive football strategy that was sure to please any crowd.

But the man that helped me most of all in high school was the uncle of my best friend, Charlie Baggett and his name was Coach Ike Walker. This was a man of distinct character. A tall man, about 6"2" and he was one of our football coaches and the track coach and the head coach of the basketball team. He was our defensive coordinator. Coach Walker taught me about successes in the history of the black man and how we contributed to our society and to our nation. I really admired his knowledge and tactics. He always got his point across to us. I would like to say "a special thank you" to Coach Ike!

Then there was Coach Kelley. He was my basketball coach along with Coach Ike Walker. This was a very family oriented man who believed in team and family togetherness. He taught us that there is power in numbers and expressed that we as players, must stick together to form a "shield of strength"! All of the above were coaches from my high school days.

When I entered college at Georgia Institute of Technology, I found it to be a totally different world outside of Fayetteville, North Carolina. It was because of their strength, knowledge and wisdom that I found my home away from home at Georgia Tech. It was there that I meet Coaches that would train me to play professional football. Coach Bud Carson was one of the head coaches. Then, there was Coach Bill Fulcher and Coach Pepper Rogers. There were a number of assistant coaches: Maxie Baughn, Ken Blair, Jerry Glanville, Floyd Reese, and Lamar Leachman.

Sorry to say, Coach Brooks is now deceased. Jerry Glanville was the Head Coach for the Atlanta Falcons and now is the assistant Coach at University of Hawaii. He was a funny and tactful man.

Ken Blair is a retired scout for the Atlanta Falcons. He was also at one point in his career a scout for the Denver Broncos. This is one of the most serious and "down to earth" coaches that I ever had the opportunity of working with. He helped me to become the "number one tackler in the history of GA Tech's football club".

Floyd Reese was an astounding assistant coach to me, he was respectful and honest. One of the friendliest coaches ever, he loved me. Lamar Leachman was one of our defensive line coaches. He had lots of funny sayings that stand-out vividly in my mind today. A big man he was! He retired as the Defensive Line Coach for the New York Giants.

I recall the revered, Coach Eddie Robinson, the head coach of Grambling University, asking me in 1971 why I chose to go to a "white" school instead of a black school. My response to him was simple. The black schools only gave me partial scholarships and I would have to work to help pay the tuition. White schools guaranteed me a full scholarship for 4 years that would pay for everything including food and rent. But, I thank "Coach" for all the encouragement he gave me regardless of where I played. He was dedicated to athletes, Thanks, Coach Robinson!

Special Thanks to: Bud Carson, LA Rams, defensive coordinator, Bud Grant, head coach at Minnesota Vikings, George Allen head coach of the Washington Redskins, Don Shula, Miami Dolphins head coach, Ray Malovasi, head coach of the LA Rams, Lionel Taylor (offensive Coordinator), Dan Radakovich (offensive Line Coach), Herb Paterra (linebacker coach), Paul Lanham (quarterbacks coach), Frank Lauterbur (defensive line coach),

Dennis Green, former head coach of the Arizona Cardinals, Jimmy Ray, wide receiver coach for the NY Jets, John Guy player personnel for Buffalo Bills, Bishop Harris, running back coach of San Francisco 49ers, Charlie Baggett, assistant head coach Miami Dolphins, Pete McCullough, head coach of the San Francisco 49ers and Lawrence Taylor, New York Giants.

And not in the least, last my buddies from the North Carolina Panthers, Pat Thomas cornerback coach for the Buffalo Bills, Reggie Wilkes, and Anthony Prior.

WHERE ARE THEY NOW?

Where Are They Now?

The kid that seemed to get into the most trouble in our group, Arnell McSwain, is today living in Tucson, Arizona. And guess what, today he is a minister and a true "man of God". One never knows how the Lord will prepare a person for His service.

Then there was my best friend, Charlie Baggett, he went on to become an N. F. L. Coach for several different teams including the Miami Dolphins. Charlie is now a wide receiver coach for the St. Louis Rams.

Ronnie McDonald is still a solid citizen in Fayetteville, North Carolina and works for Kelly Springfield Tire Company. Jerry Porter and Donald Kelly are men of God and evangelists. Donald lives in Atlanta, Georgia and I'm not quite sure where Jerry lives.

My brother, James was quite good in basketball. After high school, he went on to play for Fayetteville State and earn his business administration degree. He did really well for himself. He returned to our hometown area and married Ceretta Raines.

They have two children, James Jr, nicknamed "Jim" and Karinda, who is nicknamed "sweet girl". James Sr. has since retired from Goodyear Tire Company. He was ahead of the Minority Division of the Human Resources Department with the company. James now resides in Tennessee.

My oldest brother John unfortunately has passed. He was in a motorcycle accident and later, from his wounds developed cancer. Prior his accident he married Betty Jo and they had two children together, Debra and Leon. Both kids inherited John's flair for public speaking and energetic personality. His son, Leon was born on my birthday. Debra is a sweetheart.

Clyde Chesney, was one of the first black athletes to come out of Evan Hills. He went to North Carolina State in Raleigh, North Carolina.

Our old safety, back in high school, Dennis Monroe, lives here in Atlanta not too far from where I live. Dennis didn't go on to become a pro athlete instead; he received his Bachelor of Arts Degree in Political Science from NCA&T State University, Greensboro, N.C. and a Master of Arts Degree in Public Administration and Management from Webster University, St. Louis, MO. He later became "Major Monroe" in the United State Air Force! He now works for the government at Fort McPherson as an Intelligence Information Analyst. "The Major" and I often get together and rehash old sports and neighborhood stories. We have a great friendship and as I gotten older and I cherish the bond that reaches back so far into my childhood.

He has children and they call me "Uncle Joe"! I am proud of them both. His son is named, Theus and daughter is named, Gabrielle. They are beautiful and intelligent kids. Theus is now a barber and Gabrielle is now attending Howard University in Washington, D. C.

UNDERSTANDING GOD

Understanding God

When I was growing up, my mother always insisted that we go to church. She was taught very strict about church attendance and about learning to "give praise to the Lord". This weekly duty performed each Sunday was passed on to us.

We attended a church called, John Wesley Methodist Church located at the end of Frolic Street, on a hill. The road was nothing but mud and a hill. It was not an easy one to drive up after a good rain. It was a nice sized church, not big, but medium sized. It was brick with a tall steeple out in front of it.

Our pastor Reverent McCallum was a humble and solid man who preached his sermon as though it had been rehearsed like a play. His words will be with me until the day that I die. I must admit, that back then...it wasn't as important as it is now. But now in my adulthood and because of my many experiences I am much closer to "my Father" in Heaven.

There was a sanctified Bible Study group that was located out back of the church with a choir director, and she wanted me to join the choir and church band. I played the clarinet as I said earlier, but again, that positively was not my forte.

I enjoyed going to church. But, I did not quite understand its true purpose. It seemed to be a ritual each week. I remember thinking that it helped the time to go by. Little did I know that those simple weekly visits to the church would have such a profound affect on the life that I live today. I knew that there was a God. I knew that we, as Christians honored the Lord and tried, many times without success to obey the Ten Commandments. But it wasn't until my young adult life that I understood more about the true meaning of being a true believer and a Christian.

I'm a born again Christian now. I was baptized as a kid, but being a born again Christian now has made a big and publically noticeable difference in the way I live and carry myself. It also has made my thoughts and outlook on the right ways of living different. I now live for service in the Lord. When I accepted the Lord as my personal savior, my life changed for the better. I have such a peace of mind that it sometimes scares me.

Oh, don't get me wrong, it has taken many years and many setbacks to reach the point that I had to find my spirituality. I've probably committed more sins than the good book speaks against. There was a time in my life when thoughts and praises to God hardly ever crossed my mind. I was a child and acted like a child, and as children do, we know that God is an important factor in our lives, but it has little bearing on us as children.

Now, I praise the Lord and I'm so grateful that He has accepted and forgiven my many sins and provides me with blessings each and every day. We often take for granted the small things or circumstances that we experience. Things like, giving thanks to God for awaking us each morning. I'm so much happier with myself, now that I have found Jesus. I've always been a good, humble and kindhearted person, but during my lifetime I have made mistakes.

I have done some pretty wild and crazy things; things that I'm not proud of, but I truly believe that our experiences in life are part of the plan that God has chosen for us. I can say that I honestly believe that things happen for a reason. Life's obstacles and challenges make us stronger beings once we find out that the only way to live is the way that Jesus taught and teaches us.

I don't know about you, but I plan on going to Heaven! If you don't know by now that He is coming, I suggest that you read your Bible and understand that we are definitely in Revelations today. To make it to those pearly gates, you must find Jesus and live His way of life.

I would like to take a moment to thank the Almighty God for giving me the opportunity to live a life that has been full of experiences that have made me strong. I am attentive to the fact that nothing is more powerful than His word. Thank you, Father God for wisdom and the blessings that you have provided me. I am a success and give my love and devotion to you as my "personal savior."

I am also thankful for the many serious challenges that I faced during my life. For these are the things that have made me appreciate, the little things. I don't take for granted the fact that we are not "promised" tomorrow. Let your will be done. Thanks for bringing me to this "point of peace" within myself Father.

I understand what spirituality means and I respect it, because it is for and from you. You are Lord. You and only you have the power to grant us success in life. Success is your desire for us and we honor your faithful love and work and your care in 'breathing the breathe of life into us.

To my entire readership, live your lives in a godly manner. I pray that all of your wishes and dreams will come to be. Study your Bible, pray and believe. Be Blessed!

Secrets of Success

S – start by determining your ultimate goal in life

E – establish your priorities to reflect those goals

C – create a plan that includes room for flexibility

R – research and practice to reduce risks and errors

E – efforts lead to rewards, excuses lead to failures

T – time used wisely is an investment for the future

S – strength is achieved by confronting difficulties

O – organization, focus, & persistence gain results

F – faith in Jesus frees you from fear and doubt

S – self control is the truest test of human mastery

U – use your talents and skills as natural resources

C – challenges always offer opportunities for growth

C – change is the only constant you should depend on

E – experience exceeds all other methods of learning

S – society never owes you more than you have earned

S – success is a way of life found moment by

FOLLOW JOE'S TEAMS

Joe Harris FACEBOOK Address

http://www.facebook.com.php#/profile.php?id=1344079826@ref=name

Joe's Website:

www.GentleJoe.com

NFL All Time Players

http://www.nfl.com/players/joeharris/profile?id=HAR451815

Georgia Tech

http://sports.espn.go.com/ncf/clubhouse?teamid=59

Baltimore Colts (Indianapolis)

http://www.colts.com

http://www.nfl.com/teams/baltimorecolts/profile?team=IND

St. Louis Rams

http://www.nfl.com/teams/losangelesrams/profile?team=STL

Minnesota Vikings

http://www.nfl.com/teams/minnesotavikings/profile?team=MIN

http://www.vikings.com/splash.aspx

San Francisco 49-ers

http://www.nfl.com/teams/sanfrancisco49ers/profile?=SF

http://www.49crs.com/home.php

PLEASE READ ALL THAT YOU CAN ... LET'S TALK